noise

noise

DARIN BRADLEY

BALLANTINE BOOKS
NEW YORK

A Spectra Trade Paperback Original

Copyright © 2010 by Darin Bradley

Published in the United States by Spectra,
an imprint of The Random House Publishing Group,
a division of Random House, Inc., New York.

SPECTRA and the portrayal of a boxed "s"
are trademarks of Random House, Inc.

Library of Congress Cataloging-in-Publication Data
Bradley, Darin.
Noise / Darin Bradley.
p. cm.
"A Spectra trade paperback original" — T.p. verso.
ISBN 978-0-553-38622-6 (pbk.)
eBook ISBN 978-0-345-52273-3
1. Broadcasting—Fiction. 2. Regression (Civilization)—Fiction. I. Title.
PS3602.R342655N65 2010
813'.6—dc22
2010014910

Printed in the United States of America

www.ballantinebooks.com

2 4 6 8 9 7 5 3 1

Designed by Steve Kennedy

For Ally, who waited

ACKNOWLEDGMENTS

Many people had a part in the creation of this story. First, there are those without whose company the story simply wouldn't have come together. Aaron Leis, Ryan Cornelius, Maxwell Cozad, Michael McConnell, Tom Preston, Haj Ross, Srdjan Smajić, Barth Anderson, Mark Teppo, Berrien Henderson, and my parents, Layne and Jamye Bradley, all contributed to the collection of my ideas, and I owe them a tremendous debt for doing so.

Then there are those without whose criticism and feedback I simply couldn't have articulated the story. Liz Cornelius and Kip Nettles both deserve my special thanks.

And then there are those without whom the story simply wouldn't have seen print. My agent, Kristopher O'Higgins, and my editors, David Pomerico and Juliet Ulman, all worked vigorously to see the full realization of the story. Without them, there would be nothing.

And finally there is one who did all of these things, without whom none of it would matter. My wife, Rima Abunasser, who believed.

noise

CHAPTER ONE

We got the jump because we lived near the square. Walking distance. Slade was like most small Texas towns—it radiated outward from the old courthouse. At some point, someone had paved the original hitching yards and erected a cenotaph for the Civil War dead. There were water fountains on each pillar, each with its own inscription: WHITE. COLORED. They both still worked. There were pecan trees with dubious histories.

Livery posts, hardware stores, and hotels had clustered slowly around the squared avenue—the buildings still stared at the courthouse-turned-museum, the remnants of their painted-brick signs now protected by city codes. Those businesses were all something else now—candy shops, bars, high-end boutiques. But they had several signs each. Meyer's Pawn was the most important to us. Guitars and drum sets and stereos filled its storefront windows—the ejecta of the nearby university. Its bread-and-butter music program, mostly. Slade still lived because the university owned most of it. Sweet Pine, Siwash, and Minnie Falls, all nearby, had dried up when they were supposed to, half a century before. When Slade should've gone.

But we didn't care about instruments. Meyer's had tools, too.

We got the jump. We'd been watching Salvage for months, so we knew what to do.

We knew enough.

After television broadcasts went fully digital, people began to Salvage the analog waves. The low-end frequencies the FCC didn't sell off or restrict for their Nationwide Public Safety Network. Which was just for first responders, emergency personnel. The police.

At first, the public air was monitored, regulated in a dying-grandfather sort of way. Special needs. Suicide watch. The FCC called it the Citizens' Television Band.

In the early days, 'casts were still pirate. It took a year or so before the waves went Salvage, and you could do whatever you wanted with a broadcast antenna and a video phone. It was shortwave television. Narrow-band. Retro-hip all the way from the mechanical TVs of the Great Depression.

Modders stopped retooling old eight-bit video game consoles and mini fridges and started finding ways to improve the Salvage band. We were lucky—we didn't have to mod anything to tune in. My father's old garage TV never stopped working. Black-and-white. Eight-inch screen. It doubled as a radio.

Slade had more Salvage than most cities around it. It had college kids with plenty of money, plenty of equipment, and plenty of paranoia. They'd all been raised by the American Dream. Their teachers had told them they'd be astronauts and presidents and famous actors. They were middle class, mostly white, in a public education system that might as well have been private—they didn't know then how the property taxes on their parents' multi-story homes determined their share of "equal education for all."

They'd followed the rules, earned the grades, dreamed big and endless. And then in Slade, people handed them beer and hash pipes, had sex with them, told them it was all right not to know what the hell was going on. They Grouped themselves without knowing it—a hive-mind that kept them from being alone, that told them the bottom was about to fall out of everything they'd ever been told. Told them to expect it, to get ready. To learn about Salvage. To *trust no one*.

Even with all their money—all their equipment—it was the paranoia that served them best.

Some days, the Salvage was too thick—the anxiety, the hurriedly wired amps throbbing more power into each 'cast. Every panicked 'caster doing his best to get *his* truth through all the others'. They ended up jamming one another, like Cold War cryptographers. Numbers and catchphrases and cardinal directions squealed in and out of one another on the bad days. Some modders did nothing but jam, and their squealing tech made paranormal sounds through the TV's tiny speaker.

They were making noise. 'Casting themselves into the drone. Because it was nice not to be alone.

We had favorites. 'Casts that were stronger than others. And their owners left graffiti all over town. Stencils like stenographs on municipal servo boxes and in bathroom stalls. Wildstyle graffiti in the bar that was once a bank. Eventually, for those of us on the inside, we learned the jammers' habits, their schedules, so we knew when to listen for the *real* warnings—the real reports on what was happening. More importantly, what *wasn't* happening. With the whole country. Before the Event.

You could match graffiti to frequencies and parse new messages all across town. A sort of patchwork bulletin board that couldn't be hacked, couldn't be shut down or traced. Which is how we knew.

We had pieced together our first Plan. Knew how to get started. How to get the jump. We couldn't afford most things—guns or food or medical supplies. We planned to Forage for these, after the Event.

If we tried to steal everything, we would've just been arrested and thrown in jail. We'd be fucked when things Collapsed.

But we were going to need things. Primarily, we were going to need to get out of Slade. To get out of everything. After the Collapse, the town would get hungry. And other people would have guns.

The Collapse was like a Renaissance Faire. In my mind, they were the same. Some years before, my best friend Adam and I had gone together. Turkey legs, incense, cornets of roasted almonds. That sort of thing. We'd spent most of our adolescence playing Dungeons & Dragons—old school. Second editions from the 1980s that had been my uncle's. So we knew about trebuchets and scorpions—the difference between a glaive-guisarme and a fauchard fork. The numbers of another generation, of the Gen Xers with their hybrid engines and text messages. 14 16 15 17 17: saving throws for a first-level fighter. The unforgettable code of every Silicon Valley headcase who'd gone from twelve-sided dice to stock options and copyrights. We knew these things. We bought swords at the Ren Faire. Unsharpened things that had to be peace-bound while we stomped around the fields in the mud, paying older kids to buy us beer. They were carbon steel, which was important. They would take an edge, but that would nullify the warranty.

• • •

When word came through Salvage about the bank runs and the riots—long before it slipped through the FCC feed, before it interrupted programs and slid semi-transparently, like a snake's skin, across the bottom of every digital display in the country—we got the jump. Before anybody panicked. Salvage had been watching the silent bank runs, the electronic ones, for weeks. It knew who was going to start throwing things, in which cities, almost before the demonstrators themselves did. It knew who had been out of a job, and for how long. Who couldn't buy bread. Who had sick children.

Salvage had long since silenced the hobbyists—the 'casters who weren't up to anything more than teaching people to play the guitar, or crochet, or to understand the Bible. If you hadn't found a way in, if you hadn't cracked our codes, it was just noise. Nonsense. The only integrity behind jamming had been to silence the Outsiders first.

Salvage had become self-aware.

There were only two of us, Adam and me, but we'd need others, to grow strong, to be safe. And we'd have to either recruit them or intimidate them. So we began with swords. With getting edges.

When word came through, when the jamming stopped and everything harmonized into a layered fugue chanting the one mantra that meant the same thing to every conspiracy-head, deviant, and tagger, we ran to the square. To Meyer's.

. . . *This assumes that you will kill other people.* . . .

We left our swords on the kitchen counter—*the Faire was just beginning*—because they didn't have edges. There wouldn't be disorder, not yet, so they would just get in the way. We threw a cinder block through the front window of the pawnshop, and it lodged at a slow angle through the skin of a kick-drum on display.

. . . It assumes that a new competition for resources has begun. . . .

We were *fifteen years old again*, a wall of old toasters and secondhand TVs and abandoned jewelry an *open stall before us*. We were standing on broken glass *wrapped in Faire smells—sautéed onions and garlic*. We listened to broken music from the bar next door . . . *that there are resources yet available* . . . while we were stealing a bench grinder. We were thinking in numbers and obscure acronyms. *We were thinking 14 16 15 17 17, THACO, hit points.* We were thinking, *What are the numbers for a good strike with a sword? Which dice do we roll?*

Nothing had fully Collapsed yet. We got the jump. But it was Before, so we were just criminals. We were running, as best we could, with a bench grinder, back to our duplex near campus. The first step was to put edges on our swords, so we would be strong.

. . . primarily, the Event involved ab initio *(or has since developed) an economic revolution* . . . We didn't need a generator at that point because the electrical grid was still alive then. The Northern Lights would come later.

We were running. We were several ages at once, the present- and future-past. Stealing a bench grinder was many things at once—Ren Faires and running only two of the more obvious.

THE BOOK:

"ONE"

[1] (i) This Book assumes many things. (ii) Among them, that you are still alive. (iii) It assumes that the world has not been destroyed by fire, that it has not developed radiation flats and a meteorology of fallout. (iv) It assumes there has been a breakdown. (v) It assumes that a new competition for resources has begun; that there are resources yet available; and that primarily, the Event involved *ab initio* (or has since developed) an economic revolution.

[2] (i) The destabilization of Trade informs the competition for resources—conflict, nationalism, religion, and consciousness are all Narratives for securing these. (ii) These will be your ready tools.

[3] (i) This assumes that you will kill other people. (ii) Begin identifying the people beyond your Group as Outsiders as quickly as possible. (iii) Begin before the Event, if you are able.

[4] (i) You will need a Place, and it will require a name. (ii) Your Place is your strongest Narrative.

"TWO"

[1] (i) If your Place serves also as your residence prior to the Event, then there are a number of preparations you can make. (ii) Of course, stockpiling firearms, ammunition, fuel, preserved or preservable foods, and medical supplies is a priority. (iii) However, overpreparation can lead to disaster (cf 2.1.iv–2.1.v). (iv) If your Place is too near an urban center, then Outsiders may attempt to Forage it for supplies or shelter. (v) If your Place is overprepared, it loses mobility,

which is among a Group's most primary survival
characteristics.

[2] (i) A Group inhabiting a Place too near an urban center will
endure considerable Administrative stress in the process of
negotiating with potential Additions to the Group, for this
negotiation inevitably includes a number of necessary
eliminations—Rejections that stress the Place's perimeter.
(ii) This is problematic, for in this instance, your Group will
be forced to eliminate Rejections *before* your Narrative has
solidified against the psychological damage that can result
from doing so. (iii) A Group requires time to identify not
only itself but also its Outsiders. (iv) For this reason,
situate your Place an appropriate distance away from any
urban center. (v) Given time, a Group will stabilize its
Narrative such that Additions and Rejections will not stress
Administration.

CHAPTER TWO

The thing about a bench grinder is that it's loud, and it draws a lot of amps. The wiring in our place was old and jury-rigged as it was. Bolting the grinder onto the kitchen counter and unplugging the microwave to free up an outlet meant more than just fucking up the carpentry—we were taking a risk with the breaker. If our place was going to burn, we didn't want to be the ones to ignite it. Not yet, at least.

But we had to sharpen our swords inside, where we'd attract less attention—if any. Slade was still quiet at this point, still largely unaware. We hoped people would think we were flipping the place—college guys with parents' money, trying to dip their toes into real estate. We'd even stolen a real estate sign and paid a design major to do us up a SLADE RENOVATIONS AND REPAIR decal we could stick over the Realtor's. We put my phone number on there, just in case. We told the guy the company was to hedge our bets—to get some business going before we graduated, in case being interdisciplinary studies majors didn't pan out.

He told us to keep him in mind, for brochures and the like.

We didn't know how long we had until someone noticed the

break-in at the pawnshop, until someone noticed the sound of a bench grinder running at night. We honestly didn't know if anyone would have time to notice. Who knew when Slade would start falling apart, which would make a hell of a lot more noise than sharpening swords would.

Jo, our neighbor who lived behind and above us, wouldn't care. She knew us. She knew we did things like this. We didn't know the neighbor who lived across the shared driveway. It never came outside, even though, every night, without interruption, we could see the blue-strobe pulse of its TV. Sometimes there were shadows of movement between the insufficient blinds.

In shop class, in the seventh grade, we'd learned about tools. Which directions to move things, which machines had which tics, and which were most likely to tear off an arm. I used lines from Frost's poem "Out, Out—" to write my term paper about the dangers of the portable router.

We had to learn first aid in shop class, too. Which was fine because I was already learning it in the Boy Scouts.

The noise was a thing. The theft and the running and bolting it to the counter had been things, too. They were terminal punctuation. They were our commitment to our Plan, because these things were the last steps we could take. The final preparations. Everything else was reversible—wouldn't get us in trouble if Salvage turned out wrong. If everything quieted down, and we got jobs and suits and broke our promises to each other to live in the same town—to have wives who were friends and kids who asked us to teach them how to play Dungeons & Dragons.

But what we'd done—breaking into Meyer's, leaving footprints, ruining the landlord's counter—these were things we couldn't take back. We had to wait until we were sure. We knew from the goateed guys at the Faire's armory that sharpening carbon-steel swords on a bench grinder would ruin the machine. It created harmonics that had nowhere to go but back into the machine's bearings. And they would burn up, lock the wheels, and destroy the motor. And we knew that sharp edges were just ideas, that they fade over time, so that sharpening our swords too soon, while we were still practicing swordplay, would only mean we'd have to do it over again. That would mean *two* grinders, which we couldn't afford, and didn't want to steal. It would mean having mounted the grinder a lot sooner, when we still worried about the landlord coming around. It was impossible. If he came now, we didn't care. We were ready.

We put soft edges on the swords, which were looser ideas about sharpness than what we intended. Than what we intended to do with these edges.

We took turns, grinding and grinding, throwing sparks onto the linoleum and against the fridge. The other of us paced from window to window, watching for notice. We had every light in the house on to make it look like we were working our late-night house-flipping renovation. They dimmed, a sort of sinking light-choir, every time one of us bore down on the wheels with our steel.

We only made them so sharp. Because we had to practice, which was going to dull them. After we'd practiced, then we'd finish the ideas. We'd sharpen them fully. And we got lucky—the grinder didn't burn up, because we didn't finish the job. We let it cool, and added some lubricant, which would be enough, we'd heard, to finish the job.

There would come days, though, when we would do this by hand. With our whetstones.

. . .

What I remember most about pumpkins isn't carving them. It's the smell. Even fresh pumpkins smelled like rot to me, like bad flesh, and disemboweling them so you could insert candles felt like grabbing fistfuls of decayed sinew—the seeds like tumors caught in their own body-webbing. Roasting the seeds, with salt and oil, always seemed carnivorous, even though we were dealing with a plant.

We had the pumpkins set up on sawhorsed plywood, on the dark side of the house, where neither Jo nor our other neighbor could see what we were doing. We were screened from the next property by the backyard's mess of bamboo and sycamore trees.

Outside, in the dark, I held my sword like a carving knife. I thought about Halloweens past, about how we created glowing faces with sharp knives. How pumpkins became jack-o'-lanterns. About what I wanted faces to look like. About what I had to do to a pumpkin to get what I needed to know about striking someone in the head with a sword.

It took practice, slicing into the pumpkins instead of simply knocking them from the plywood.

We also used watermelons, which were important because they made "the sound."

Later, we finished the idea. We finished the edges and burned up the grinder. Adam put all the pumpkin seeds we'd picked from the plywood on a baking sheet. Added salt and oil, because there was no sense wasting. Not with what was coming. We had to become accustomed to doing carnivorous things.

. . .

Killing people outside a grocery store is more than it seems. It is also collecting baseball cards.

It is an entire pack, a box of packs, too large to *steal*. You must simply *take* them, right in front of the assistant manager who only let six students in at a time because our junior high school was too close, and we all stole too many things. After the first card, there is the next, and the next, an entire loose-leaf photo album that isn't yours. And somehow it means something, even though baseball bores us, because it meant something to our fathers. It is a stack of talismans we'd rather not understand. And they stack and stack.

So do the people, when you kill them.

I was twelve then, and there were three of us: Jon, Chuck, me. In the wooded lot behind our development, we had a fort. A copse of trees, really, at the soft end of a floodplain, where the city had installed an extra storm drain, right in the trees, leading to the main culvert nearby. The culvert was only slightly more important to us than the fort. It was an open-topped, cement trapezoid, and it was horseapple fights, experiments with aerosol spray and butane lighters. It was access to a second-place, between our housing development and the next, between and below privacy fences. It was an underworld where we sold scraps of stolen *Playboys* and *Clubs* and *Penthouses* to one another. It was where we got beat up. It was our Place.

The city's failed drain became our coffer. We wiggled the calcified service "key" out of its brackets under the iron lid and finished the job that runoff had started: sealing the drain and its ground-level vents with mud, sticks, anything that would move downstream. We made it our own Charybdis.

A neighborhood grocery store moved in a year or so later, absorbing the majority of our field into its parking lots and facilities. So we formed a Plan.

On Friday nights, we would sleep over at Jon's house. His parents let us watch unscrambled late-night cable and stay out as late as we wanted. As long as we stayed in the neighborhood. Which was fine with us. The neighborhood was all places to us.

Through the culvert, through the fort, through the unmowed grass at the edge of the lot—the grass as tall as we were—we took the field back piecemeal. We read teach-yourself ninjutsu manuals and practiced moving invisibly and silently through the grasses. We destroyed the store's decorative shrub-lighting with clubs from the fort because doing so with the baseball bats we had used in Little League, on team Yellow Jackets, felt wrong. We threw bottles into the lanes, and nails—anything we thought would make grocery store life generally unlivable.

By day, before and after school, we took back the store. We stole medicines, mostly, because they were small and expensive. But we also took anything else we wanted: pens, lighters, a whisk. Anything small enough to escape the ceiling's bubbled, black security windows.

And eventually, we stopped stealing and started taking. A gallon of milk, a mop. A box of baseball cards. What twelve-year-old would walk out with a gallon of milk? The store's bigger problem was the other kids, those stealing bags of candy to sell on the blacktop at school during lunch—the managers always caught them. We were never caught. Our combination of force and paranoia was stronger than guilt and stealth, which never worked.

We dumped everything in our coffer, used or not. We were most amused by just destroying what we'd taken.

Adam hadn't started stealing until college, when he dated a punk girl without realizing it. He didn't know until months afterward, when she told him that what they'd been doing, stealing together, was dating.

We were force, and paranoia, moving through the culvert along University Avenue toward the store where Adam and I bought ramen noodles by the shipping crate and boxes of mac-and-cheese and soda. We ate these things while we played Dungeons & Dragons after work. We had never stopped playing.

Word had slipped through the FCC, and things were unraveling. We chose this store because there was a pharmacy across the street, and we intended to target both. We parked Adam's truck beside the unused loading dock of the mostly empty shopping center a few blocks away. We used the culvert to move along the avenue to get to the store because we thought the swords would provoke a fight, if people could see us. Not everyone was being strategic. Some were getting high on disorder for its own sake, with better odds than not that the police wouldn't even show because they'd be controlling panic elsewhere. Most of the National Guard that watched the armory along the highway had been deployed overseas.

The swords had taken their edge on the grinder. We had hacked through whole melons earlier in the morning.

WHIS.PER had been quite clear. It was the only thing he ever said, and he said it behind a mask, behind an assumed name, into the tiny lens recording his 'casts.

Overcoming the aversion to violence is best effected through disguise.

It was the only thing he ever said, over and over, and most

jammers left him alone for it. We painted the tops of our faces with shoe polish, and masked the bottoms with doctored swaths of our darkest T-shirts. I remembered from mine and Jon's and Chuck's ninjutsu manual how to turn a T-shirt into a ninja's hood.

"Did you decide?" I asked him. Overhead, sports cars with exhaust mods gargled furiously past.

"Levi," Adam said.

"Yeah? You sure?"

My heart was realizing the task at hand, pumping so hard my field of vision was twitching.

"Yeah. Sure."

I'd chosen my new name already, had chosen it right away when I'd seen the wildstyle directive in greasepaint on the commuter-lot dumpster. There was a sigil as homage to WHIS.PER's Rule, his 'cast frequency in faux-stencil. The new message was around it. No vowels.

Thy shld tk nw nms.

Hiram.

We were stalling. "All right," I said. "Nothing that won't fit." We had backpacks.

"Yeah." Adam's bright blue eyes drew in what dusk remained. What flotsam would move downstream to collect in our coffer at the bottom of the field.

... *You are not yourselves.* ..., I said. Just walk right out and disappear into the grass.

The Plan was simple. We wouldn't *steal*, which is paranoia—we would take, which was force. Things were falling apart faster than we expected.

We wouldn't go inside the store. Inside was chaos. If there had been more of us, maybe three, we would have. The disorder didn't scare us—it was electric, new. Being someone else in a familiar place with new rules. Unpunishable rules. We figured that, inside, people would be shoving and running. Punching, stabbing, shooting for what they wanted. Or simply because *other* people wanted something. Not *what* but *because*. Because they could now. Those that survived, that fought their way out or slipped through the tidal surge from the bread aisle to the baby food, would already be tired, would already be hung over on their own adrenaline. They might be wounded, or out of ammunition, or unarmed.

We were mostly correct. So we crouched behind an overgrown holly bush and spotted. We were looking for targets, but it was already dark, and most of the store escapees were not pushing carts but sprinting with armloads. We wanted singles, and it was hard to tell who was running with who else. We didn't want to fight. Especially not more than one person. That was the point.

From inside the maw of the entrance, from between what shards of glass still held to their frames, through flickers of flashlight and a shouting drone, things crashed. Banged. We heard a shot.

We had already drawn our swords.

"This isn't working," Levi said.

. . . You are not yourselves. . . .

"Can you see?" I asked mechanically, craning my neck, tugging at the shirt around my face. I had the same view as Levi.

"Yeah. No."

"Maybe we should try the pharmacy," I said.

Levi looked over his shoulder, peering through the curled holly leaves. "Same there."

Every instant, more targets slipped by. More canned meat, batteries, isopropyl alcohol. More pockets filled with butane lighters.

My heart was still hammering. I was thinking in fragments, atemporal, simultaneous things. *Ghostbusters,* T-ball, staring at panty lines in lecture halls. I was sweating my clearest thoughts onto the leather wrapping the sword hilt. I was shutting up and thrumming forearms. I was my best friend. I was still afraid of being arrested.

"Tell me to do this."

"What?"

"You have to fucking *tell* me to do this. I'm not doing it—you need me to do this. Say it."

He wasn't sure.

"Say it."

He wasn't sure.

"Don't fucking *look at me*. Don't. Fuck."

. . . You are not . . .

"Take one down." *. . . yourselves.*

I was on the outside, farther from the bush than Levi.

"I need you to take one down."

I didn't even stand. I just swung the sword into a pair of running shins. Chips of things hit me in the face.

The problem with practicing on watermelons is that they don't have bones, even if they do make the noise—a noise you don't want to be surprised by.

I remembered T-ball. Team Yellow Jackets. Hitting a baseball with an aluminum bat stings. The ringing, in your ears, is not what you think it is.

This, of course, was not the Plan. The force of the running shins against the sword knocked me out of my crouch, away from the bush.

Adam shouted. It was his voice, and not Levi's—I could tell.

But I couldn't hear him over her screaming. Her face was right up against mine, after all.

"What?"

"What the *fuck*?" he whisper-shouted. He was looking around frantically, ducking and rising. He looked like he was preparing to steal something, which wasn't the Plan. We came to *take* things.

Around us, between the cars in the parking lot, people kept running, kept dropping things and pulling at one another and looking back. The store was still making noise.

It sounded like traffic laws in the nearby intersection were losing force. Cars had become weapons, and some sounded stronger than others.

"Stop screaming," I told her, dazed on my back. "Just . . . stop."

Levi shuffled over.

"Christ, you didn't even *ask* her," he said.

I turned to look at her. She had stopped screaming, and her eyes were trying to look up, inside her forehead.

"Well, neither did you," I said.

. . . Do not panic. . . .

"Jesus. Jesus."

Jesus.

"What's she got?" I managed to ask, sitting up. In the darkness, her blood looked like the oil oblonging the parking spaces.

Adam was touching her, tentatively, like she was a wounded animal. Something he intended to study, but not yet. Not while it could still spit and spray and blast adrenaline into his stream.

"Levi," I said, . . . *best effected through* . . . not looking at her, *"what's she got?"*

Thy shld tk nw nms.

"Uh . . . uh"—he rummaged—"diapers, matches . . ."

. . . *disguise.*

I started gathering things and shoving them into my pack.

"Okay, look at me now."

"What?"

"Now you can look at me."

He stopped and looked. The folds around his eyes had cleared themselves of polish.

"I think . . . I think we need to always look. At each other. Afterward."

He looked back down. "Okay."

When we'd sold candy, to raise money for cleats and flags and dues to the YMCA, I had practiced in the mirror.

"Hello."

Morally . . .

"I'm selling candy to raise

. . . *these Outsiders . . .*

"money for my T-ball team, the Yellow Jackets.

. . . *are natural enemies.*

"Would you like to buy something?"

. . . *They are predators.*

In the end, though, you bought all the candy yourself. Or your parents did. You took what you needed to fulfill the team's need. You paid.

• • •

The girl was a brunette, or red-haired. The shock had gotten her. She was still breathing, but her eyes were closed now.

I stood up and leveled the point of my sword at her throat.

"We don't want to hurt you," I practiced.

I couldn't remember what to say next. What we had agreed to. People ran around me, hammering the oily pavement in the shoes they'd thought best for sprinting through the End of All Things.

Levi stood up, sword down. Playing Bad Cop.

"But we need what you have," he said.

I looked at him, waited until he looked back. "You can give it to us."

"Or we can take it."

"Do another one," I told him. "I need you to do another one."

He looked around, crouching by reflex. An insect poked mid-thorax. "Wait, are other people . . . is anyone else killing?"

"We don't want to kill anyone," I said. "Remember?"

We stacked our cards. Cross-legged in sweatpants. A Saturday afternoon at Jon's house. We traded what our parents had bought for us and checked values in our price guide, hoping to sneak bad deals past each other.

We took our turns at bat, wincing before we even reached the T. Afraid of it, of contact. It always hurt to connect the aluminum bat with the ball, and we couldn't hear our dads through our regulation safety helmets. They were usually too big, but they still pinched the cartilage in your ears. Things still hurt when you kept *your eye on the ball*, and did someone say *good hustle*? You couldn't be sure, standing before the T.

This would hurt, so you couldn't *be yourself*. You couldn't *most importantly, have fun*. You were not yourself in your T-ball disguise. You were a Yellow Jacket.

There is no I in team.

The ringing in your ears is not what you think it is.

THE BOOK:

"TWO"

(cont'd)

[3] (i) If, conversely, your Place is situated far from any urban center, is relatively inaccessible, and has available resources, prepare as much as possible as far in advance as possible.

I.

"PLAN"

[1] (i) You will need a Plan. (ii) This Plan must include a Place, a Group, and an Event Exit Strategy.

I.A.

"PLACE"

[1] (i) The principles behind selecting a Place are simple. (ii) It should be remote yet not excessively so—later, Trade, exploration, and recruitment will become vital. (iii) Your Place should offer security. (iv) That is to say that while it may not be equipped *ab initio* with ramparts, palisades, or the like, it must at least offer a high degree of visibility of the surrounding territory. (v) In the event that you attempt too late to secure a Place and the available locations offer neither fortification nor visibility, then you must settle for something discreet, preferably a cave or other such enclosure. (vi) In the unfortunate situation that, post-Event, you have neither a Group nor a satisfactory Place, you must immediately gather the necessary resources and equipment to sustain and defend yourself. (vii) If you

possess a skill set that would make you a worthwhile
Addition to a Group, such as small electronics or generator
repair, husbandry, medical training, or engineering, then you
need only concern yourself with sustenance and defense.
(viii) If, however, you lack a skill set with which to Trade
yourself to a Group, then you must hoard, secure, and
transport items of worth, including medical supplies,
ammunition, or essential knowledge.

[2] (i) Your Place will require a name. (ii) With the other
territorial, cultural, and discursive landmarks of your old
"self" dislocated, Foraged, or destroyed, you must very
quickly project yourself into your new Place, which, for a
time, will be all Places. (iii) A Place is a form of extended
consciousness, in that it delimits and defines perception. (iv)
Motivated perception, in turn, delimits the construction of
your world.

CHAPTER THREE

When we first found out about Salvage, skipping class in the coffee shop, we became obsessed. We stopped playing Dungeons & Dragons. We became like soldiers, disciplining each other: class, homework, work, Salvage. We took notes, indexed broadcasters and jammers, and followed directions. We asked around town, over and over until, finally, someone sold us a crib sheet for two hundred dollars. A dictionary of stencils and graffiti, for what was being written into Slade. We studied it, tested each other. We began compiling our version of the *Book*, which was the manual. Holy Writ. The collected Salvage manifesto, assembled from the snippets and fragments and bits of useful information buried beneath all the broadcast noise. Everyone had a different version, which was good. If we all followed the same framework, we'd end up competing.

We dropped classes to lighten our homework. We couldn't drop out altogether. We were taking financial aid, and without it, we'd have to work too much. We wouldn't have time for the *Book*.

We bought books secondhand, so there would be no record of purchase. Things like *FM 21–76, Department of the Army Field*

Manual: Survival, The Anarchist Cookbook, The Survival Bible. I still had copies of *The Official Boy Scout Handbook* and *Unintended Consequences.* It had been five years since I earned my Eagle Scout Award. I was the youngest in the troop to ever do so.

We weren't far from the house, a duplex with only one livable half. We lived in the annex, tacked onto the old place in the 1950s, but we stockpiled things in the old half, the 1890 half: some books, a picture of Thoreau, a fifty-pound bag of salt we'd taken from L. D. Pizza, where we were delivery drivers.

We only had to make one turn, then onto Broadway Avenue, the civil artery that wormed past the road to the university on one side and to the square on the other. But we had to shoot one car to make it. One of the people we stacked in the parking lot, before we moved to the pharmacy, had been carrying a snub-nosed .38. Unloaded. Ammunition in its pockets.

People were driving in whatever direction they wanted, particularly college guys in lifted pickups and sports cars. They were smashing what they could reach with aluminum bats, standing upright through the T-tops of their Camaros or kneeling on the wheel wells in the beds of their buddies' pickups. People were stopping and swerving and smashing things.

We had an open lane—only needed to go ten blocks—but someone was scared in front of us. Weaving between lanes, avoiding bottles, hoping to be ignored. There weren't other immediate threats around us then, but we couldn't take the chance. A lot could happen in ten blocks.

I pulled the .38 from my pack, loaded it, and rolled down my window. I looked at Levi and waited.

He watched the road, waiting. Eventually, he turned and stared at me.

"Remove it," he said.

I nodded. Refixed my mask. I fired one shot at the old Buick in front of us, which was nearly driving on the median, trying to avoid abandoned cars in the other lane.

For such a small gun, the explosion made my ears ring. My head rushed with blood, and the recoil jammed my elbow against the window frame. I wasn't ready for it.

The Buick's rear window iced over instantly. Clouded, webbed, a tiny hurricane eye just off center. The driver moved fully onto the median, rocking the car, and veered onto the correct side of the road. We'd been driving on the wrong one.

One of our early exercises had been the erection of a training dummy. We used scrap wood and parachute cord and a set of pulleys we got from the Army/Navy Surplus Store next to Meyer's. We'd take turns, puppeting the dummy for each other. We'd swing it in all different directions, at different heights, between the giant sycamores in our front yard. Twenty feet away, cars raced down the road. We lived directly off Broadway, our yard elevated some ten or twelve feet. We could hear the bell tower on campus; we could see the spire on the old courthouse downtown.

The boards we used for the dummy's arms splintered easily, but we didn't care. We kept at it, lacerating our own arms on the things's shards, keeping track of our progress by the disappearance of our wounds.

Adam gunned his truck up our driveway, throwing gravel like gunshots, tiny, popping bombards that clacked against the siding. Of our place and the neighbor's. Jo's place was an above-and-below two-unit behind the small parking lot in the back, curtained, in places, by all the bamboo growing against the fence.

We could see the cat, even in the dark, as we skidded past our porch. It wasn't one we recognized, and it dangled, hanged from the throat, from a length of our parachute cord. Cars raced and braked out on Broadway. People flashed in and out of sight on the sidewalks, streetlit threats running different places.

I looked away from the cat. I was still wearing the shirt around my face.

We unloaded the truck. Our cats, Fluff and Edmund, were safe inside, under my bed.

I stared at them.

Jo didn't answer her door.

She was a vegetarian, and she invited us over sometimes for tasteless spelt pasta or to smoke a bowl. She wasn't old enough to buy beer, so we'd bring it. We'd sit on her balcony and get drunk and talk. We would stare down the driveway, watching the cars pass in artificial river-motion. Everyone going somewhere else, underground, along the asphalt water. There was an IOOF cemetery down the road, below the road, where indigents lived in crypts like naiads in the riverbed, waiting for the current to deliver something useful they could drag down.

We would get drunk and talk. We would make sure to say things like "Kierkegaard," "chic," and "not just sex, but something spiritual, too." She hadn't liked Adam's punk, and I'd been slow to realize she was a lesbian.

"Keep a watch," I told Levi. We'd pulled the shirts from our faces. He turned and looked out over the balcony rail.

I knocked again.

"Jo," I said, not too loudly, "it's us."

I saw the pulse, darkness inside against darkness out. The peephole shutter-blink that anyone could always see. No matter what was going on outside.

"It's us, Joely. It's all right."

She opened the door, an inch—the length of chain still protecting it.

"It's us."

"Is it *just* you?" she asked.

"Yeah."

"Someone was walking around your place."

"Yeah."

"They're saying—"

"What, on the news?"

"Yeah, they're saying that—"

"Fuck the news."

"It's time to go," Levi said.

"We're going, Jo."

"You fuckers," she said, closing the door. She slid the chain free and opened the door. "This is really happening. All your . . . shit."

"Where's your pack?" I asked. She had a bandanna tied onto her head, a college-girl bonnet-looking thing. She was wearing cargo fatigues and a tank top, which is what she usually wore.

"Did you pack a pack?" Levi asked.

"We told you—"

"I've got the fucking pack," she said, turning into her dark apartment. "Jesus, what are we going—"

"Don't panic, Jo."

"We have a Plan."

THE BOOK:

"TWO"

SEC. "I," SUBSEC. "A" ("PLACE")
(cont'd)

(v) The strengths, weaknesses, and needs of your Place will, in time, reauthor your Narrative of self and align your existential concerns. (vi) Your Group will develop a new cultural discourse (a new culture altogether), and it is this new discursive entity—this interactive phantasm—that will orient your cognitive development into the new era. (vii) Naming your Place imbues it with cognitive force. (viii) Naming your Place alters it from inert territory to a raison d'être. (ix) It is advised that you name your Place prior to the Event, which will enhance the motivation to reach it, should you encounter difficulty executing your Event Exit Strategy.

[3] (i) Do not share the location of your Place with Outsiders, pre-Event or post.

I.B.

"GROUP"

[1] (i) Establish your Group before the Event. (ii) A Group offers the obvious advantage of collaborative survival, in that Members of a shared ideology and motivation become, very quickly, one social organism implied by their Place. (iii) Discuss the Group, the Place, and the Event often. (iv) In this regard, by the time the Group inhabits the Place, it will already imply a history, which is an essential component of your Narrative.

[2] (i) Your Group must first include Members who can contribute. (ii) While it may be argued that physically noncontributive members can accentuate your emotional state, including them will be a calculated risk, for as your Narrative develops, this accentuation may weaken, depending on the success or Failure of your Place. (iii) Further, physically noncontributive members consume resources and create new theaters of concern.

[3] (i) However, physical contributions can include such areas as entertainment, social cohesion, and Narrative development. (ii) This means that Members may be considered contributive if their skill sets include musical talent, brewing or distillation, esoteric horticulture, storycraft, or other such knowledges and skills. (iii) These contributions imply equipment that the Group must acquire and transport. (iv) Such transportation is a risk, but it is a delayed investment that will later enhance your Narrative and strengthen Place-Narrative.

[4] (i) Despite these possibilities, no Group can sustain Secondary Members (the aforementioned) without adequate Primary Membership (those who can endure physical labor and who can and will fight). (ii) Secondary Members do not mature into Primary Membership until the Group Arrives at the Place and establishes its first Day. (iii) For this reason, your Group should focus primarily on Members who can effect a successful Event Exit Strategy.

CHAPTER FOUR

Where will we go?" Jo asked. She was standing at our front window, peering out between two finger-lifted blinds.

"West," I said, cinching a strap on a duct-taped duffel.

"What's out west?"

"A Place," Levi answered.

Jo turned around. "What? Fuck you. Tell me where."

I stopped. "You don't understand. It's a *Place*. It's our *Place*."

She lit a cigarette. We didn't like it when she smoked inside.

"This commando shit has got to stop," she said. "A place, a *place—this* is 'a place.' "

"No—" Levi started.

"Adam—"

"Levi," I corrected her.

"*What?*"

I rolled the duffel aside. She was standing up; I was kneeling, a now taskless arm draped across my knee. We looked chivalric. I'd played knights, in mine and Adam's D&D games, who knelt like this.

"Jo," I said, "*this* is not a Place. Adam is Levi; I am Hiram. We have to be because this won't be easy. *That*"—I pointed at the window—"will kill us. You can't be yourself in all this because it won't work."

"Everything has changed," Levi said.

She looked from one to the other of us. Scared.

"We will survive," Levi said. "We'll keep you alive. We like you, Jo."

"We'll start everything new."

"What?" she said, covering her unease with a drag from her cigarette. "So you're going to, like, start a tribe, and I'm the one who will bear your warrior sons, or something like that?"

"Don't be stupid."

I looked at Levi. "Give it to her."

He shuffled off to the laundry room. There was a maintenance door in there, which we used to get to the 1890 half.

She sat down. "What the hell?"

She was starting to panic.

. . . *Do not panic.* . . .

"It's okay."

"What about the police? This is like, just like, a hurricane or a disaster or something. You guys need to calm down—this will be over in a few days."

"There aren't enough police," I said.

We bounced a little, on the floor, as Levi walked back in. The pier-and-beam foundation had spots, like funny bones, that answered steps in one place with bounces in another.

He handed her the *Book.*

"The police have families, too. Friends. They won't be police much longer."

She looked at Section "One."

"And the National Guard is mostly overseas. *If* they come back, there'll be too much for them."

"This has been coming, Jo. You've watched Salvage."

She looked up. "With you guys. Smoking pot. A Friday night in Slade. That's just . . . underground art or something."

A car roared past outside, full of screaming somebodies.

I stood up and motioned to Levi, to the gear.

"We'll give you an hour, Jo. Read."

"You don't have to come."

"We won't make you come, but you should. Cities are the most unsafe."

Levi slung a duffel over his shoulder and headed for the laundry room. I turned on our little black-and-white TV. A fuzzed, diagonal portrait straightened itself, jammed. Which was, in turn, jammed. I listened for a second to the fugue. To the noise. I couldn't make out even one uninterrupted message. Pictures flashed and jarred. Someone was shooting something live on a hand-mod—I could see people running. The lights were off on Reunion Tower.

It didn't matter. We had Salvaged what we needed.

Jo had her head in her hands, the *Book* in her lap.

"You'll need a new name," I told her softly. "You'll need to be new."

"All right," Jo said, half an hour later. "Okay."

"Okay?"

We were sitting cross-legged in the living room. Levi was manning the black-and-white, searching the frequencies for something useful. I had turned on the big digital in the corner, but muted it. They were talking about the bankruptcy declaration.

About the Emergency Farm Bill. The ticker on the bottom of the display scrolled only one message.

Remain indoors. Follow law enforcement instructions.

Over and over, like a Salvage 'cast. An ouroboric ribbon noosing the talking heads.

"When can we come back?" Jo asked.

"We don't know," I said. "We're not planning on coming back."

"What if we can?"

"Depends."

"On what."

"Which Place is better."

She picked at the carpet. "You have food?"

"We have everything."

"Medicine?"

"Jo—"

"Do you have fucking tampons?"

"We'll get some."

"We have everything."

"All right."

"Okay?"

"All right."

Jo was lying on her back, staring at our ceiling. We had dozens of things to stare at in the living room. We'd made it into a sort of geek-boy clubhouse, a throwback to classic movies we watched when we were little, when we were younger: *The Goonies, The Explorers, Hook, Conan the Barbarian.* We had a dress form. A fishing net. An emptied barrel-of-monkeys hanging hook-armed everywhere. We had a vintage lava lamp.

But Jo stared at the ceiling.

We were waiting for the Lull.

"What kind of a new name?" Jo asked.

Levi looked over his shoulder. First at me, then Jo.

"Any kind," I said. "Something new. To you."

"Did you two write the *Book*?" she asked.

Something squealed on the black-and-white. Levi went back to tuning it.

"Some of it."

She propped herself on an elbow. "Who wrote the rest?"

"Lots of people."

"From Slade?"

"Some. The *Book* is different for everyone—people have collected different things, from different places. Some things come through Salvage."

"Which would be different everywhere," she said.

"Yes."

"How did you come up with your names?"

"You want me to help you pick one?"

She lay back. "Yes."

"Mary."

"Why 'Mary'?"

I watched Levi scribble a note.

"You can do anything with that name," I told her.

She folded her hands over her belly—the tank top had exposed it, her dimpled navel gasping. "Why not 'Eve,' then? It was first."

"Fine. Eve."

"No," she said.

Remain indoors.

"Mary."

. . .

"What are we waiting for?" she asked.

One of our cats had come out from under the bed—the calico we called Fluff. I was scratching her head, staring at the digital. There was some problem near Louisiana. The Republic of Texas guys were prepared for this. They were going Gestapo out in the pines, which was bad. East Texas still had racial problems. Nothing I needed to note in the log.

"The Lull," Levi answered.

"Which is?"

"A lull," I said, laughing a little.

Mary slapped the back of my head.

"You are such an ass."

"We'll go right before the Lull," Levi said, reaching for another of her cigarettes. She'd been sharing them with him. I watched.

"Why before?"

Levi took his hand away from the tuning knob, slowly, as if he'd just set a fuse, or a trap. The screen dithered between two broadcasts. One looked just like the feed I had on digital, but the ticker had been modded to scroll Eliot's "The Waste Land" instead of civil instructions. The other was a still room-shot of two students reading to each other in turns, one from Machiavelli's *The Prince*, one from a tourism guide to New York.

"Found it," Levi said.

"You found it?"

"Found what?"

"It's a tourist guide this time. Barely fucking heard it."

"Found *what*?"

"Shut up a minute, Mary. Are you far enough between?"

Levi still held his hands in the air, hovering over the black-and-white as if summoning it to levitate. As if he might wave the broadcast away if he moved.

"Yeah," he said. "Seem to be."

"Between?"

"Broadcasts," I told her. "To find Fat Chance, you have to find New York. It's always set up with some local 'caster, somebody different each time. Always somehow New York. You have to be between frequencies, between whoever's been chosen and the next schmuck."

"Sometimes you pick the wrong one," Levi said, scooting away from the TV so we could see it better, "go higher instead of lower."

"How do you know? If you missed it?"

"Transcripts of the 'cast show up around town."

Static popped through the broadcast, jammers trying in vain to crack the 'cast. Always. But no one ever outgunned Chance's local 'casters and their overclocked amps. We guessed that Chance's agents chose his people by measuring their equipment.

"Everything began with the first man," a girl's voice said.

"Around town? I don't fucking—"

"Mary, shut up a second."

"Hasn't used White in a while," Levi whispered.

"We shall name him 'Last.'"

"Fat Chance is a girl?" Mary asked. Quietly.

"No, Mary."

"Last began with dirt and a plywood shanty, both of which he found."

"We think 'Fat Chance' is a Place—a Group, actually."

"He made everything from nothing else."

"We're not sure if it's actually in New York."

Levi was taking notes. Some of the best lines in the *Book* came from Chance. Sometimes codes, crib-sheet updates. Sometimes it was just gibberish, bullshit. Noise.

It had never been a story before.

" 'Nothing else' included the circuit boards and cables from a disabled

computer. It also included the tube and capacitors from a discarded monitor, a keyboard, a mouse without buttons, and an inkjet printer. From nothing else, everything began."

White, we knew, after albino marijuana. New York White. Stories about it growing underground in the sewer when everyone flushed their seeds. Blind, and clean, and perfect in the stench. Most thought she was a metaphor for a first-place, a rally point, that Fat Chance had laid in, waiting for the Event. For the Collapse. Everybody's first-place was based on what we'd cracked of her code. What we'd all cracked and stenciled and spread around town. Around the state. Country. Some said world.

White meant everything was going okay. According to Plan. A girl, a Place, a Plan. Some called her Snow White. The Cracker. The Bitch, The Whore, The Angel, The Score. The Ice Queen. The Wet Dream.

Adam and I called her "Hope" if we didn't want anyone to know what we were saying. In case there were other Salvagers around, and we weren't sure.

"Last began everything with the book in the shanty. It read, 'This assumes many things.'"

"She sounds hot," Mary said.

"This assumes many things."

The audio popped and fizzed. The 'cast was over. Chance's 'caster eased up on his amp and let the jammers collide, washing the waves with the pent-up shouts, catcalls, and codes that couldn't get through White.

THE BOOK:

"TWO"

SEC. "I" SUBSEC. "B" ("GROUP")

(cont'd)

[5] (i) Do not allow your Group to grow too large. (ii) Further, you
must elect (or someone must assert) Leadership. (iii) This
Leader is the final, authoritative voice during the crucial
period before a Group Arrives at its Place. (iv) Post-Arrival,
decentralize your Leadership—by force if necessary. (v)
Would-be autocrats who resist decentralization are warned
that they risk expulsion, rebellion, even banishment or
death, for as the Narrative establishes itself, Leaders are
primary targets for blame-placement. (vi) Because the early
stages of establishing a Place involve many difficulties,
losses, and discomforts, it is inevitable that blame will
require placing. (vii) Leaders are warned that they will
likely carry this blame, and as the majority of Places will
Fail, most Leaders will lose either their lives or, at the
very least, their chances for survival.

I.C.

"EVENT EXIT STRATEGY"

[1] (i) Your Event Exit Strategy is the sequence of maneuvers that
will Evacuate your Group to its Place.

[2] (i) That only some will execute an Event Exit Strategy is to
your benefit—those who do not will generate the disorder
from which you can Forage a number of useful supplies. (ii)
Your first inclination, post-Event, will be to assemble your
Group and Evacuate. (iii) Disregard your inclination.

[3] (i) Your Event Exit Strategy begins with the convention of the
Group in a first-place. (ii) The first-place is meaningless—it
is a location only. (iii) You and your Group should take
pains not to become attached to the first-place, as it may
weaken the Event Exit Strategy.

[4] (i) If you are a lone Member who must travel to join your Group,
proceed immediately to your Place or nearest rendezvous
point. (ii) The First Phase of the Event Exit Strategy
involves unacceptable risk to lone Members. As such, this
phase is restricted to a Group-sanctioned excursion Party.

CHAPTER FIVE

Why before the Lull?" Mary asked again.

Levi finally lit the cigarette. With the upper half of his face still polish-dark from the First Phase, and the black-and-white gleaming in hot, phosphor contours along his profile, he *looked* like Levi. This was a new person, a smoking person. We'd beaten the shit out of Adam and left him ducking in the parking lot, watching for cops.

"The Lull is a contradiction," I said. "We have to get the jump."

Mary was refolding her headkerchief in her lap. "What does it contradict?"

Levi muted the black-and-white. "Those who think to get out are going to wait until things get quiet. 'Til people start running out of steam."

"Everybody's high now," I said. "Smashing and speeding and what the fuck else."

"Eventually, they'll get tired," Levi said, "and the misinformed will make a break for it."

Mary looked up. "So—"

"Think about it," I said. "Everything's quiet, suddenly you're the only one racing out of town."

"Bad idea," Levi said. "You become game, prey. Something to chase."

"Or," I said, "you think you're getting the jump, but you just end up in a mob of evacuees. Everything starts over, but this time you're fucked—stuck in your car on some road across town."

"But leave before the Lull," Levi said, "and sure there'll still be Outsiders gunning around, but the odds are on your side."

"Sickest numbers game ever," Mary said.

Or the best.

"How can we tell when it's before the Lull?"

We.

"It'll be a narrow window," Levi said. "We think there'll be a sudden rise in civil activity: sirens, emergency lights—that sort of thing. But it'll be a false dawn. By that point, most Groups in town will have mobilized. The civvies will just get in everyone's way, so they'll be removed."

"But you guys are Salvagers, too, right? I mean—"

"Mary," I said, "beyond this room, there are only Outsiders. Predators, enemies. Targets. But it's a two-way lens."

. . . Trust no one. . . .

Mary's phone rang. We tensed, watching as she pulled it from her pocket and set it against her jaw. She looked at us, hesitant, guilty-looking. I got up to monitor Broadway.

"Hello."

Smoke was rising from the square.

"What?"

Someone was upset on the other end of Mary's connection. I could hear garbled panic-speech.

"*What?*"

Somebody must've Placed the courthouse. With enough Members, it could be impenetrable. But no land.

"Wait—"

Which meant everything they needed would have to be Foraged. In an urban center. Eventually, it would become a death camp. And there was the matter of all these churches, if you stuck around in town. They'd find you. Prearranged mobs. Armed and hungry and divinely ordained.

"No, Ruthie, just wait," Mary said. "They won't come in."

She had been staring at the ceiling, at the fishing net, staring phone-call distances at nothing. I turned around.

Now she looked at me.

"Just stay there," she said into the phone.

I talked like she wasn't there. Like Mary wasn't standing there.

"Is this a bad idea?"

Levi looked at Mary. This is how things worked. A decision was external, every time. Someone else's doing. Beyond Group-thinking, even. This was Place-thinking.

"I don't care if it's a bad idea," Mary said, moving back and forth from the window to us.

We ignored her, facing off. Generating thought. I had my sword in my hand, the .38 in my pocket.

"You'll have to Forage the place quickly," he said.

"What?" Mary tried to get between us.

I grabbed her shoulder, jammed her into the stance. Made her stand and stare. We were three, now. "Stop thinking," I said to her.

She swallowed.

"Does she have special needs?"

"Like what?"

"Medical."

"No. I don't . . . no."

"Dietary?"

Mary shook her head. She looked down.

"Look, Mary. You have to look. Later, you can look away."

She lifted her chin. We were scared. We were standing stiff. Centripetally locked. Now, with someone on each side, there was nowhere else to look. Before, Adam and I had looked away. . . . *Look twice.* . . . Before we knew how important the look would be. Now we were geometric. . . . *Move once.* . . . Trigonometric. Algorithmic. The science of sharing burdens.

"If you're going to help her," Levi said, "you have to help Hiram. Do everything you're told. Make her do everything she's told."

"Okay."

"Do not correct the operation."

Her eyes were like Adam's, back outside the grocery store, drawing in what would flow downstream. Into our own Charybdis. Into the coffer in the mud at the back of the field.

Mary put on her jacket. Zipped it up. She capped her head with the kerchief. When Levi finished repainting my face, he handed the tin of polish to me, to use on Mary.

She stopped my hand. "Do you have white?"

Levi headed for the laundry room.

"I will be white."

I went to get a different shirt. For her mask. Mary stood, lit by the black-and-white on one side, by the digital on the other. Standing. We hadn't told her to move yet.

. . .

We couldn't risk the truck—we would need it later. Mary's had four doors, which meant two extra risks, so we'd use mine.

Levi corked the last cocktail and handed it to Mary. She had four cradled in her arms. Rag-tongued wine bottles filled with oil and gasoline. We couldn't smell the fumes through our masks. We checked the walkie-talkies, which we'd bought, legitimately, from the Army/Navy Store next to Meyer's. Months ago. We would switch channels, up to the next prime number. Up to the top, then back again. Only on cue and cue-back. The radios were for the Evacuation. We hadn't planned other operations pre-Evac. I had a crib sheet in my pocket.

Mary adjusted her burden.

"Everyone between us and Ruth is our enemy."

Gunning the engine is a daydream. It is sunroofs, waxed paint, and artificial slick on the wheels. It is a better sound system, with deeper bass than the tinny stock setup you have now. It is a girl in the next seat, wearing a cross expression. For now, she is freebasing on your adrenaline, on the *nothing will happen* that counterbalances her better sense. Later, you will be the boyfriend who is stupid and troglodytic, with an affinity for the accelerator she doesn't understand. A boyfriend who is too easily jealous, who gets angry for idiotic reasons. A pulp thriller she can read to her friends, who will share the mythic disdain. But for now, you're her ticket out, out, out because who the fuck understands anything anyway? Who the fuck knows the zeitgeist but her?

. . .

. . . Do not render aid to Outsiders. . . .

Gunning the engine is rendering aid to Outsiders. Because you go your own way carefully. It's the Outsiders, with the exotic needs, whose ways must go in fire and exhaust, in peripheral stare-downs with too-close drivers in other cars. Nerves of steel and cool. To be the one who can do *the thing*.

. . . Remain in your vehicle as long as possible. . . .

It is a synaptic equation, going fast. It's the press, the delay, the calculated explosions under the hood. Even alone, driving to the same somewhere as always, gunning is always what it *could* be. The rehearsal, the performance. A mastery of escapes, races, demolition. The stories in your head. . . . *The journey is only a synaptic ribbon*. . . . Of being the guy with the fast car. The music and the bloodstream. The stories you can never finish before you think another thought. Before another thought thinks you. . . . *Only the journey to reach it is real*. . . .

Gunning the engine is every drive home always. The revision. The all-at-once, the compaction of instants into that same. Slow. Press. All instants at once. How you dropped her off. How you got it there in *thirty minutes or less*.

It was fifty miles per hour down Mulberry Street. The wormhole-speed compacting time so that Mary and I were only out on the roads as long as we had to be. It was her being quiet, not correcting the operation. It was the mob loitering ahead in the road, near the commuter lot, where a sigil and WHIS.PER's Rule were— something Solomonic, painted onto a dumpster in the shadow of a pecan tree. If the mob disabled the tires, Mary and I would be alone and insufficient.

My pulse makes sound the same way woofer cones do. Disturbing the air. Disturbing the better sense in my bloodstream, the brainless coup of pocketed blood in ready organs. In muscles that do things all the time without me. In strategic pumps and stutters. Not sound, but force. Noise.

. . . *Take no chances. . . .* , says one of my brains.

Gunning the engine is . . . *do not hesitate to use your vehicle as a weapon. . . .* It is the sports car I drove to my senior prom, the tackle boxes filled with miniature lead warriors, the trips to Adam's to game all weekend. It is Dungeons & Dragons on a Friday night, playing characters of both sexes, to be sure we got the story right.

It is the history I've created for Jo: her first date with a boy named Leslie—an idea that had promise: switching the names around, coming at the confusion from a different direction. It is a forced smile at the hand on her thigh. An accelerator-mindtrip out of the past, out of his car. It is what I think it was like, being Jo, being gay.

It is a day trip to Slade, before Adam and I graduated. It is the long, long trips out west, where I went instead to follow Her. I left Adam in Slade. I watched tumbleweeds and contrails and come-and-go dust devils in the red, red dirt.

It was the loitering mob, a many-legged thing without a brain, with only one long, spinal nerve. The sense of being from ass to forehead.

It was the will of our Place, drawing us across 327 Texas miles.

"Now," I said to Mary.

She lit the rag in one of her bottles and rolled down the window. My ears followed the breeze, sucked of their pressure by the force of the wind. Mary touched the burning rag to another and undid her seat belt.

"One per side."

She knelt on the seat, and I jammed my fingers beneath her waistband, grabbing a fistful of fatigues and underwear to keep her steady. She stood up completely, out the window, swayed by the wind, and my arm thrummed.

I was not thinking. I was White Mary's tensed ass as she gave her guttering bottles to the loitering mob. The shambling thing underfoot.

I was the splintered fence-board in my fists at the fort. I had been dipped in a coffee can full of gasoline, and I was a flaming torch in a swordfight with Chuck—

Mary fell into the seat when I jerked her back in.

—Jon made the mistake of emptying the can onto Chuck's last flame. A recharge. A suddenly thrown thing disking gasoline fire onto the dead leaves around us.

I did not follow Jon when he ran to the culvert. I stood with Chuck and looked for the first time on a wall of fire.

Gunning the engine was Dopplered screaming as we compacted and vanished down the road through campus. They hadn't laid spikes. But if they had, at least they couldn't mob the car anymore.

I picked up some speed before we rounded the turn to Ruth's apartment. At the corner, I slipped the car out of gear and cut the lights. I had the .38 in my lap. Mary had a bottle in one hand, a lighter in the other.

This street was darkness, deep in Cement City, the low-income underworld where college students took advantage of rent-controlled housing. Ruth lived in the Zodiac Arms. In a building called Taurus. It looked as if the grid had already died here. No one on foot, no one else driving. We were being cased.

Mary directed me to the building. I drove right up onto the

lawn, right outside Ruth's door. We weren't taking any fucking chances.

I turned the car around, pointed it back at the parking lot. Mary waited for me to get out and lock the door. She followed me, bottles tucked under her arm. We planted our backs against Ruth's door.

"Try calling first," I told her. "It's quieter."

Mary turned, ducking, as if even I needed to be kept from the conversation. I watched the other apartments, looking for that dark-on-dark blink, the giveaway that someone was looking back.

"Okay, we're here," Mary whispered.

I could hear Ruth's digital murmur in Mary's earpiece.

"No, it's just us."

"Okay."

Mary turned and looked at me. Her eyes were blue, like Levi's, simple and staring. As blue here as they'd been between her roadside fires on Mulberry Street.

Mary, Mary, quite contrary.

"She's coming," she said.

I nodded. "Pull the mask off your face, so she can see you."

She tugged it free.

"Look at me."

She looked.

"What you did was right."

Ruth's apartment was a studio. The popcorned ceiling was peeling free. The baseboards were misaligned, that mystery rental-unit grime scummed into their cracks. Formica. Dark fluorescent bulbs. A futon and a papasan chair. She and Mary were whispering hurriedly in the bed nook, assembling Ruth's pack.

There were textbooks everywhere with yellow stickers on the spines that read USED SAVES. Easels. Soldering irons and rivet punchers and a small jeweler's torch.

I checked again through the window and slipped toward the nook.

"You work with metals?" I asked.

They stopped and looked.

"Yeah," Ruth said. "I'm in sculpture."

She was thicker than Mary. Long hair with untrimmed tail-like ends. She wore a labret. Her left arm had been fully sleeved with tattoos.

I looked at Mary. "Two packs. One for her, one for her metals gear."

Mary nodded and went back to stuffing underwear into a messenger bag.

I looked at a Monet print over Ruth's bed. The only flowers in this cement underworld.

"Hey," she said. "Thanks."

"Hurry."

THE BOOK:

"TWO"

SEC. "I," SUBSEC. "C"
("EVENT EXIT STRATEGY")
(cont'd)

[5] (i) If your Group is sufficiently large that Cells of three or more members share urban centers, then each Cell should independently execute the First Phase of your Event Exit Strategy prior to Evacuation. (ii) Otherwise, only one Cell should attempt the First Phase.

[6] (i) Do not ignore signs of the impending Event. (ii) It is far better to gather in the first-place, preparing for the Event, and find yourselves mistaken than not to gather at all. (iii) Should you find that you are not with your Cell or Group when the Event occurs, collect yourself and any others for whom you are responsible and proceed immediately. (iv) Arm yourself before you make your way to the first-place. (v) Once you begin the journey to the first-place, do not stop. (vi) Do not render aid to Outsiders. (vii) Do not gather supplies, no matter how available they appear. (viii) Do not be alarmed by civil disorder. (ix) Do not be alarmed by violence. (x) Alter your route to avoid areas of obvious risk. (xi) Remain in your vehicle as long as possible. (xii) If Old Trade has completely Collapsed by this point, do not hesitate to use your vehicle as a weapon. (xiii) In the event of complete Collapse, law enforcement and military personnel are likely not to be the social allies they once were. (xiv) Regard them and their instructions with trepidation.

[7] (i) The first-place is your priority. (ii) It is your identity. (iii) "You" do not exist. (iv) You are an extension of its

consciousness. (v) Only the journey to reach it is real. (vi)
The journey is only a synaptic ribbon. (vii) All roads lead to
the first-place. (viii) Do not panic.

[8] (i) If you must reach the first-place on foot, pay constant
attention to your surroundings. (ii) Avoid open areas. (iii) Do
not let Outsiders come within reach. (iv) Run, if you must. (v)
Use violence if you must. (vi) Do not let weapons fire
discourage you. (vii) Do not run in straight lines.

[9] (i) Avoid public transportation unless you are capable of
seizing and operating the vehicle. (ii) Under these
circumstances, remove or incapacitate other occupants. (iii)
Do not take Outsiders to the first-place.

CHAPTER SIX

house of Cards, this is Party. Do you copy?"

"Who the fuck is this?"

"Party, this is HOC. Go ahead."

"Target is in custody."

"Spook? Are those ours?"

"What fucking target?"

"Channel cue."

"Cue-back."

I jumped channels.

"HOC, this is Party. Do you copy?"

"Copy, Party. Go ahead."

"Coming home."

"Copy. Code check."

I pinged Levi with a flurry of dots and dashes. "S E C U R E," so he knew. So he knew we weren't under duress.

"Copy. Did you encounter resistance?"

"Affirmative. We neutralized a mob at WHIS.PER's Rule and Mulberry Street."

"Did you take casualties?"

"Negative."

"Copy. Look twice. Over."

"Copy, HOC. Over."

I started a different route back. We couldn't take chances with the Mulberry mob. Likely, they'd be lying in wait now. More road spikes—real ones. Some guns. Something bad.

Those that hadn't burned.

I could see Ruth looking at my sword in the backseat. I hadn't cleaned the blood from it yet. The edge had taken a severe curve when it hit that girl's shins.

I could see, in my rearview mirror, that she had spacers in her earlobes.

Mary was holding the gun, staring through her window. In the glow of the dashboard instrumentation, she looked spectral. A ghost-face hovering, something you could see only in reflection. Like in the dark, if you said *Bloody Mary Bloody Mary Bloody Mary* into the mirror. Late at night, or in the afternoon with towels shoved under the doors.

You had to say it alone. You had to stand alone with the dark and the mirror, knowing that what you couldn't see was you not seeing. You saw yourself not seeing yourself, seeing Bloody Mary, a ghost in the darkness.

But you never did it alone. You cheated, took a friend, took Jon, since it was his house, the corridor bathroom between his room and his little sister's. You saw Jon not-seeing, which was better than not-watching yourself.

Mary stared through her reflection, not seeing Ruth in the dark seat behind her, staring at the blood.

Maybe Mary never knew about the *Bloody*. She was just Mary, seeing things in the dark.

I braked. Hard. Our collective guts clinched. Gunning the engine was everything in the right direction. Braking was never good.

There was something new on the Wailing Wall.

I pulled alongside the cracked parking lot and cut the lights.

"Keep a watch," I told Mary.

She rolled down her window.

"What's wrong?" Ruth asked.

Mary waved a hand, eyes on the dark. "Hush, Ruthie."

Mary had a little lamb.

I picked up the walkie-talkie, turned it down, since Mary's window was open.

"HOC, this is Party. Do you copy?"

"This is HOC. Go ahead."

We had a quiet channel.

"I've got some new material on the Wailing Wall. We're going to have a look."

"Any activity on your perimeter?"

I looked at Mary. She shook her head.

"None so far. We'll be on watch."

"Copy. Be quick."

"Get a pen. I'm going to read it to you."

"Stand by."

I looked out my window. Without the instrumentation glaring against the glass, I could see pretty clearly. Earthmovers and excavators and piles of concrete lay arranged at right angles. Sundered rebar clawed at the air. The developer hadn't broken up The Noodle House's old foundation yet, though the building itself had been cleared a month ago.

I turned and looked sideways at Ruth, speaking through my mask. "Hand me the binocs."

"What?"

"Binoculars. Give them to me."

She did.

"Party, this is HOC. Go ahead."

I could see through the gaps in the old block, see the mid-century buildings on the other side of University Strip. The coffeehouses and bookstores and the bank that had been spared demolition and gentrification by a zoning debate. Most were closed. No doubt Big Red, the tavern around the corner, would still be open. One-dollar wells, two-dollar domestic drafts. "You call it" special—half off for the end of the world. Ladies get in free.

But we were out of sight, and the Strip's parking lot had been gnawed to shards last week. Amid protest. There had been a candlelight vigil for the 1920s-era brickwork nested in haphazard patches throughout the asphalt. Like continents. Those that made it right up to the end of things.

The bricks would be repurposed downtown. Twenty dollars to donate one with your inscription to the city.

The burned-out shell of Marco's was ahead to our right. Students had chained themselves and made short films and ultimately burned the place down. In protest. Taking their bar before it could be stolen by the developers. Salvagers had quickly cleared out what paneling and tables had survived the fire. Marco's was a grimoire of codes and stencils, carved and markered everywhere inside. Some on top of others. A Salvage speakeasy. Adam and I had bought our first crib sheet at Marco's.

It had one wall left, which would be the last to go before the faux-colonial prefab came in. Before gas lamps and fake stucco made ghost stories out of the old muggings and vandalism. The fights. Mainly, it would be last because it was a single condemned wall—thanks to the arson—and needed special civil architects before it could be brought down.

The Wall had once been a mural. Civilly funded graffiti art, when a crop of liberal city planners replaced the old conservative farming guard. Eventually, it became several murals. Then a paint-and-mortar notepad for taggers and Salvagers. We'd relied on it often, getting frequency shifts, 'cast schedules, and heads-ups. We were Masonic, gazing through layers of useless tags at an esoteric palimpsest, finding what we needed in pieces, looking through the Salvager's camera obscura for perspective on the impending Collapse.

"It's from Chisolm, HOC. A signing-off. Stencil and crib-speak."

"Copy, Party. What's the message?"

I translated the vowel-less script: "'Northern Lights on the Nine. Follow the grid—'"

Something slammed into my door hard enough to pop my ears. I ducked and gunned the engine, the wheel already arced to turn us around. The wrong way down a one-way road. The right way now.... *Motivated perception, in turn, delimits the construction of your world....*

I realized, as our car tailed itself around, tires screaming—announcing itself through the gaps in the Strip, straight through to the shambling crowd outside Big Red—that there hadn't been an explosion.

Breaker.

Whatever it was had been thrown, or launched somehow.

Breaker.

I flipped the headlights back on as I overcorrected. There was somebody in front of the car. We weren't moving fast enough to do any real damage yet, but I pushed him off his footing—the baseball bat in his fists followed him down. By the time I slammed again on the brakes, we'd already passed him a body's-length under the axles.

I remembered to depress the clutch. So the engine wouldn't stall when the RPMs died. I tugged the sword past Ruth. I had to kick the door to get it open.

"Out, Mary," I ordered.

Its fleece was white as snow.

She didn't hesitate.

He was getting up. A Hipster. A Strip-rat in old jeans and an undershirt. He had Salvage cryptography markered all over his clothes. A chunk of concrete sat nearby, where I'd stopped the car originally.

When the demolition started, they'd had nowhere to go, the rats. The Strip was all places to them. Panhandling, playing music. Trading crib sheets for baggies and cigarettes.

"Party, do you copy?"

He wasn't getting up. Just rolling into better, flatter positions on the asphalt. A living cipher, straight from the derelict heart of Slade Salvage. Trying to get his esoteric shit together.

I wanted his information.

"Give us your clothes," I said.

"What?"

"Give us your fucking clothes."

"Fuck you, man. Give me your fucking car. I need a ride."

He was drunk.

"You can give us your clothes, or we can take them."

"Party, do you copy?"

"I don't, I don't . . ."

I knelt to take hold of his foot. To remove the boots so I could get the pants. "If you don't cooperate—"

He kicked at me, just enough to wobble me out of my stance.

"Neutralize this," I told Mary.

She had already drawn the gun, was already, in her own mind, shooting him over and over and over. She was standing, breathing, a ghost with a gun in the darkness.

Bloody Mary, quite contrary.

He made a go of getting up.

"I need you to neutralize this."

I could do it. But I needed her to do it. She needed to do it.

"Party, what's your situation?"

"Jo! What are you doing?"

I stood, too, pacing him up. He stuck his hand in his pocket. He wasn't even a sword's-length away.

"Mary."

Its fleece was white as snow.

"You did the right thing."

"HOC, this is Party."

"Go ahead, Party."

"Saying again, last lines from the Wall."

"Copy. Go ahead."

" 'Follow the grid to the yellow-brick road.' "

He paused. Swearing out loud into the House of Cards, our house, for the both of us. Northern Lights were not good—neither was the yellow-brick road. Slade was on a timer now. Chisolm's last go before getting out of town. Pitting the Salvage hive-mind against itself. Phantom Cell Structure. Against Slade itself.

Because once called out like that, by any one Salvager to all others, to really, really get things going, they would all play along. They'd waited so long—some preparing, some fomenting, each with eyes only for the Event. And what they'd be allowed to do, once the old rules were really gone. Chisolm was setting them after the municipal infrastructure—after the electrical substations. Salvagers would obey—each alone, and all together. The drone of their disconnected ideas too loud to realize they're all one thought. The ghost in the Salvage machine.

That was the thing about Salvage—it knew something about everything, but it had no idea what it was doing.

"Copy. Is everything okay?"

"We're coming back."

"You did the right thing," Levi said. Shutting the laundry room door behind me. I walked past him with Ruth's packs.

Ruth stood in the kitchen behind Mary, looking at Levi. She hadn't wanted to stay in the car—had wanted us to let her out, to let her go—but we ignored her. Drove her. Passing a pair of brawling gangs on State Street seemed to explain things to her well enough. She was quiet the rest of the way.

"I know," Mary said.

I stepped up behind him. "Look, now, Mary. Look at us."

She looked, her blue eyes black in the darkened kitchen.

"We needed you, and you came through."

"Well, I needed you—"

"You don't understand. 'We' includes you."

We all stood there. Levi and I had only rehearsed this on each other. To make sure Members knew their acts of violence were necessary. Were appreciated. Were Group and Place and staying alive.

I cleared my throat. "Let's get out of these paints. Take your mask off, Mary."

We weren't violent then. There is a difference between paint and not.

"You can have the first shower, Mary," Levi said. "You earned it."

"Don't ask her about tonight," I told Ruth. "Don't bring it up when she's not wearing paint. Don't bring any of it up."

I opened the fridge. "How about a beer?"

"Yeah. Thanks."

I smiled, looking, I imagined, less like a guerrilla hero and more like a raccoon. She was our guest, Mary's guest—I wanted to be cool. Wanted it to be cool. I knew how she felt.

"You can ask anything else."

"Okay."

She didn't look like things were cool.

"You want an ashtray? You smoke?"

"Yeah. Thanks."

"Why do you call her Mary?"

I stacked the Strip-rat's clothes by the door. Levi turned back to the black-and-white. The rat had been carrying a code in ink between his shoulder blades that we hadn't encountered before: the code for the frequency of a magazine in Morse code—continuous broadcast. It must have been new. Levi found the frequency, and the ringing, arrhythmic Morse began chirping into the room. There was no video.

"Was it worth it?" Ruth asked from the couch.

"What?"

"Taking his clothes."

Mary walked in, dabbing at her wet head with a SOUTH PADRE ISLAND beach towel.

"Yeah."

"What news?" Mary asked. "Word on the Lull yet?"

Levi was transcribing the broadcast magazine on a stenographer's pad. One of several we'd taken from the office at work.

"Not yet," he said.

"What'd you get from the rat's clothes?"

I looked at Ruth. "You're going to need to make a decision."

"Why 'Northern Lights'?"

"Because when they burn, at night, it looks like the Northern Lights," I said. "Lots of weird colors, not much sound."

Ruth snorted. "Some secret code that is."

Mary tucked her legs up under her. "Chisolm wants to burn all the substations at once? Kill all the electricity?"

"After they do the Nine, maybe."

"Which one's the Nine?"

"It's on the east side of the square, near the municipal center."

"It looks like an old brownstone house from the outside," Levi said.

"I've never noticed it before," Ruth said.

I smiled. "Exactly."

"Substations are eyesores," Levi said. "So the city planners disguise them to maintain property values. Make them look like houses, office blocks—that sort of thing."

Against one wall, underneath the old display case my mother had used in her wedding shop, we had stacks of photocopied civil documents. Codes, edicts, census information. We'd paid almost a thousand dollars for it. Five hundred each, after financial aid

had disbursed last spring. The new city planners were into beauti-
fication. Substations, brick walks, renovating the Strip. We had
it all.

Levi pointed at the stack. "Read up if you want."

"Why's it called 'the Nine'? Is that code?"

"No, it's just substation number nine."

I didn't say that we'd thought it was code, too. At first. Before
we bought the stack.

Ruth lit a cigarette. Mary did, too.

"Why will they start there?" Ruth asked.

Levi was transcribing the Morse 'zine again. He wasn't
listening.

"Center of town," I said. "Once the Nine goes, it'll be easy for
Salvage to move to the closest others. They aren't far—a couple
miles apart each. Once they've killed Three, Four maybe, transformers will start blowing all over town."

"Which means fires," Mary said.

"Yep. They want to start downtown to get the municipal
center to start drawing from its generators. The sooner those
die . . ."

"What's the grid? The yellow-brick road?"

"The grid is the grid, the electrical grid."

I heard a bit of the 'zine 'cast. It was a schedule. I wasn't sure
what for. I'd missed the first part. Levi was being very quiet.

"And what's with all this terrorist shit? I thought you
conspiracy-heads were about surviving, not . . . revolting."

"They're speeding up the process. Salvage isn't *supposed* to be
out to *hurt* anybody—it's *supposed* to be a *reaction* to the Event—
but the sooner it cuts the systems that most people rely on,
the sooner the unprepared will start dying off."

The girls just looked at me. Some jammer got ahold of the
frequency, started 'casting numbers into the code. It would take

a while before we knew whether they were random or another code themselves.

"The sooner they start dying, the easier it will be for the rest of us, the prepared, to survive."

"Three, ought," the jamming-code said, crackling through the black-and-white's tiny speaker. The 'casts were feeding back on one another, making theremin sounds between the dots and dashes and the numbers. The voice sounded like a robotic child's.

"That's the theory, anyway."

"One."

The girls smoked. Mary looked pointedly at the ashtray, tapping her cigarette into it. She wasn't looking at me. "What's the yellow-brick road?"

"Four."

Fluff stretched herself on the carpet. She blinked at me, her affronted green eyes staring, judging. Edmund—the other cat, the black one—looked, too, sitting beside Ruth.

"One."

"It's Broadway," I said.

"Fucking . . . Can't this asshat jam something else?" Levi said.

"Five."

"Wait, *Broadway Avenue?* Like, outside the front door?"

"Yeah."

Ruth looked at the window. The blinds were drawn.

"What happens on Broadway?"

"Nine."

"It's fucking pi," Levi said. "Give me a break."

"Nine."

"Wait."

"Nine."

"What happens on Broadway Street?"

"That isn't pi."

"Nine."

"What was that schedule, Levi?"

He looked at the window, too. "The fires."

"Nine."

We were quiet for a moment.

"Shit, everybody to the back of the house. Pick up the goddamn cats."

THE BOOK:

"TWO"

SEC. "I," SUBSEC. "C"
("EVENT EXIT STRATEGY")

(cont'd)

[10] (i) When the Event occurs, monitor news programs in constant
shifts. (ii) If such programs are unavailable, allow
capable Members to perform reconnaissance in graduated
distances from the first-place. (iii) Reconnaissance
operatives should follow the same guidelines as Members
approaching the first-place on foot. (iv) You are watching
for clear signs of the Collapse of Old Trade. (v) It is
likely that looting, violence, arson, and vandalism will
either accompany or precede the Collapse. (vi) When it has
become clear that civil unrest has outpaced local
authorities, you will begin the First Phase of your Event
Exit Strategy.

[11] (i) As uncontrollable disorder becomes the new rule of law, law
enforcement and military personnel will necessarily
abandon their cohesion to tend to their own Groups and
families. (ii) At this point, though your Group is now in
considerable danger, you may Forage without fear of legal
reprisal. (iii) Should you begin the First Phase while the
rule of law still prevails, then your Group is Criminal.
(iv) Contrary to popular anarchic thought, your new
society is unlikely to develop order, and therefore
operation, if it takes its infantile steps criminally. (v) The
Plan is a reaction. (vi) It is not a catalyst; neither is it a
revolution.

I.C.I.

"THE FIRST PHASE"

[1] (i) The First Phase is the acquisition of supplies before the Evacuation. (ii) This acquisition necessitates at least three Members. (iii) Additional Members can strengthen the operation, but care must be taken not to expand an excursion Party beyond the tolerance of its central, task-based Leadership. (iv) It is primarily an exercise in vigilance.

[2] (i) The excursion Party must only include Group Members who are capable of and willing to commit violence against others. (ii) Members who are willing yet incapable may assist as an Auxiliary Demolitions Party.

[3] (i) Contrary to the Narratives of contemporary media, committing acts of severe, debilitating violence against others is monumentally difficult for all but a small percentage of society. (ii) As such, overcoming the aversion to violence is best effected through disguise. (iii) Party Members should adorn themselves with masks. (iv) They should wear clothing or armor that obscures their skin.

CHAPTER SEVEN

Calm down, Ruth," Levi said. "You have to make a decision."

I glanced at the others in the circle. Each sat cross-legged on a different rug. Some of the rugs looked Middle Eastern, some Navajo. Mine was simply a giant rug-picture of a wolf. It had been provided.

The others had their chins up and their eyes closed. Cassandra, the evening's hostess, sat in the center, small votive offerings to each of the four corners around her. North, South, East, West—she appeased the compass before we all sat down to become spiritually lost.

"You have to decide that the 'you' you know is mistaken. It is occluded, screened by the smokes and muds of our contemporary society."

I closed my eyes. I wanted this to work. Wanted to experience *something*. Spiritual.

"Your totem animal is the better you. The wild and natural you. You must decide that it is a better 'you' than you are."

I didn't know how these ceremonies went. I had just followed a flyer on the wall at The (D)rip, the coffeehouse on the Strip.

PAGAN FELLOWSHIP, ALL WELCOME
UNITARIAN UNIVERSALIST CENTER, 112 NORTH MAIN

Would there be sex? I knew terms like *sky-clad* and *Great Mother*, but I'd spent too much time in Southern Baptist churches growing up. I wasn't an atheist yet. Not then. I liked the . . . respectful anarchy of the neo-pagan movement. I'd read about it on the Internet.

I tried very hard.

I was losing patience. When the Nine blew, Ruth went into hysterics. The mobs hadn't broken her, not the trip here or the Strip-rat. What we'd told her about Salvage. None of that. It was hearing the explosion, feeling the fizzed air pressure, like a TV on mute that you can still *feel*.

The explosion hadn't been as concussive as we'd thought, but afterward, we could hear transformers groaning all up and down Broadway. Bright lights, big city, and then they popped, one at a time. That was it for the yellow-brick road. The Wailing Wall had been right, and we were left with darkness and smoke.

After a minute, we led the girls back into the living room. Opened the blinds, let them look at the Northern Lights. Mary stood at the window, uninterested in Ruth's fit, her no-longer-painted face occasionally violet. Green. Red. The substation burned silently, throwing its alien-hued fires a hundred feet or more in the air. We could see them clearly, even though we were on the west side of the square.

For now, there were no screeching tires, no shouting crowds, no one running down Broadway. There was the silence and the light and a Slade riding the first wave of its trip-fantastic into a very bad near-future.

For now there was Mary at the window, Levi setting new batteries into the black-and-white. Colors phased across the wall, across our upright suit of imitation armor, hammered out of tin. Across our gaming console. Across the map of West Texas we'd tacked onto the wall—the Place noted with a giant safety pin, likely farms nearby that we could Forage marked with multicolored pushpins.

"Ruth, you can shut up, or you can leave," I said.

"How long will it last?" Mary asked.

"Five minutes. Maybe ten," Levi said.

"*What?* Fuck you! You can't throw me out there."

"The fuck I can't."

"Why is it so colorful?"

"Fine, I'll take my shit and go. You psychos can play army all you want."

"We're not sure. Salvage just knows what happens, in most cases, not why."

"No, your stuff stays. It's ours now. It belongs to the Group."

"What *group*?"

Mary turned around, limned by the light like some holy nimbus. I looked at her for a minute, expecting something meaningful.

"This is fucked up," Ruth said. "I'll call the police."

She picked up one of her packs. I couldn't remember which it was—her personal gear or the metalworking tools. I stood up. Behind me, Levi had stopped working on the black-and-white.

He handed me one of the swords. Mine, judging by the blood. He had stabbed, not swiped, and the wounds had sucked his blade clean.

"Drop the pack." I was standing in front of the door.

"Or what? You'll kill me?"

"Ruth—"

"I can't believe you brought me here, Jo. What the fuck!"

"Yes," I said.

"Yes, what?"

"Yes, I'll kill you."

She was calmer now. Remembering, I guess. Thinking of the rat in the street by the Strip. "You're not wearing your . . . your paint."

"Ruth, sit down."

"Drop the pack, Ruth."

"We have to stay together."

"You have to make a decision."

I convinced myself that my totem was an eagle. I was into eagles. I was part Indian. An Eagle Scout. I made fetishes out of grapevine and raffia and gave them to my friends like some shaman.

The eagle was a better me than me. My totem.

Afterward, we went to Cassandra's house. The guy on the Navajo rug was her husband. I hadn't caught that. We smoked pot and talked about gaming. They gamed, too, and thought I might like to join.

Was that it? It's just what I decide? The totem is what I decide?

Was that spiritual? I was being open-minded.

"Open Minds," Beginner's Zazen, all welcome,
Thursday, 7:30 PM, Room 255, Auditorium Building

What did it mean that I had bottles of unrefined frankincense at home? A baggie of Dittany-of-Crete. One mandrake
root. A mortar-and-pestle I'd bought in an online auction.
The Southern Baptist Convention disallowed female preachers,
and incense came in colored sticks from the drugstore, not in
roots and weird powders. What I knew was clearly not what
I knew.

I made my own potions, my own blends, finally a fucking
shaman. I followed recipes from a book and highlighted words
like *empower* and *release*. I had done this in the evening when
Adam had class. The first year. Trying to figure things out.

Ruth let Mary sit her down. I lowered the point of the sword.

"You need to keep an open mind about this."

It was quiet, even after the Northern Lights faded. The university
would be dark, too, but they had generators. We had one, but it
wasn't for Slade. It was for later.

The jammer had disappeared from the Morse 'zine. We
weren't sure when the next substation would go.

"All right," Ruth said.

"All right."

"I get it."

"It's all equal. Once we get out."

"Yeah."

"Nobody's going to tell you what to do, except the whole of
the Group."

"I get it."

"But—"

"I get it."

"You get it?" I got up and grabbed the Strip-rat's folded clothes. I tossed them onto her lap. "You get it?"

"Yeah."

"The Group is everything. Outsiders are our enemies. Predators. People who will take what we have, however they can. They're going to become desperate."

"I get it."

She tucked her hair behind her ears. Mary was sitting cross-legged next to me, between me and Levi.

"Do you have family or something? Out . . . there? At this place?" Ruth asked.

"Something."

"Where is it?"

I looked at Levi.

"If we tell you, you have no choice. You either come along, or we have to neutralize you before we leave."

I looked back at Ruth.

"I get it. Where is it?"

Even Mary was looking.

I pointed to the safety pin.

There.

"Is anyone else coming?"

"No."

"What about, like, your parents?"

"Don't ask about our parents."

"No one else is coming."

The fires didn't start immediately after Salvage cut the power to the yellow-brick road. We waited for the schedule 'zine, the

Morse bulletin, to re-'cast. From the beginning. Broadway had some time left. The fires would be burning out in the Red Light District now. There were only rumors of prostitutes there, but everyone had a story about "seeing" one. The gangs were there, and they'd been first with the fires. With one another.

The square was a column of smoke, but without any wind it only went upward. A wall with nothing to enclose. It *was* the enclosure. Whoever had Placed the old courthouse was in some shit now. I stood on the porch, in the shadow next to the 1890s door, while Levi did a check around the house. The smoke was only some two or three hundred yards distant. I didn't hear any shouting from there anymore.

There was a part of me, the part that had crawled through tunnels between storm drains, that had loved the Teenage Mutant Ninja Turtles in Johnny-come-lately TV syndication, that wanted to step through that smoke, into a land of the dead. To make sense of an underworld utopia. I was in the seventh grade when we read Edith Hamilton's *Mythology*. The River Lethe, Nepenthe, Cerberus, and Hades. I sometimes confused the Greek and the Roman. I didn't understand the living fascination with a world of perfected dead.

The traffic had mostly died. The intersection of Broadway and Sycamore, on the other side of the house next to ours, was filled with smashed, abandoned, and gun-shot cars. It made a good roadblock.

The new Slade was a quiet one. The delinquents were out of sight.

"Clear," Levi reported quietly.

I nodded from the dark. "All right—get your two hours, then." Rest in shifts. Just like the night-watch rotation of every Party in every game of every D&D campaign we'd ever played. We usually got bored around sixth level and rolled up a new Group of characters. Sixth level brought the real power, when you could *do* something with your mages and dwarves. With your paladins.

Things started to suck with too much power, so we always started over.

"Two hours," Levi repeated. He climbed the steps. Looked at the smoke with me for a minute.

"Girls are eating."

I nodded.

"What do you think about Ruth?"

I looked at him. "Works metals. Soldering and all that."

"That justifies the pain in the ass. I guess."

I smiled. "How'd we end up with two lesbians? In this?"

"Ruth, too?"

I looked at him funny.

"Yeah, I guess so."

"Yeah."

I was fourteen the first time I gamed. I had been invited. Adam and I had a mutual friend from our junior high school, so we met. Adam was the Dungeon Master. I brought Chuck and Jon—

"You all right?" Levi asked.

—I played a rogue. I named him Kirn Steelhawk, and he wore masks and took false names. I played well, so I was invited back— Chuck and Jon weren't. My mom didn't like that I was playing Dungeons & Dragons. Said it was satanic. Even though I'd just experienced God in the empty sanctuary of our church. I'd convinced myself of this. Desperately. I'd told my youth minister, and we'd all prayed our thanks together.

I'd even read *Mythology*, so I knew the difference—

"I'm all right."

• • •

Mary lay down next to Levi. In Levi's room, off the living room. It was smarter for them to rest in the same place. If one heard something, he or she would wake the other. They wouldn't have to wait on Ruth and me to hear it, too.

Ruth was sitting cross-legged in the middle of the room, reading the *Book* by the black-and-white light. There didn't seem to be much coming from Salvage now. I was waiting for a newscast, something stripped from somebody's still-working digital, but Salvage was just repeating the rules. Being as clever as possible. Now and then, somebody would sign off. A Group on its way out. Clearing the noise.

I pulled out the earpiece. Let the cats have the rest of the salt-broth in my bowl of ramen. We sometimes added cayenne, just for something different. Not this time. We weren't wasting spices now.

Nothing outside the windows when I looked. The same.

The thing about that book, about *Mythology,* is that, in the backs of our suburban, middle-class, Southern Baptist minds, thinking of dumb, classical ancients and their miraculously ingenious architecture, this was just as good—a different Bible. It was from a time when people didn't tell sex jokes, or raise taxes, or know what stars were. We thought. They were stripped-down humans, primordial savants making brilliant things, waiting to collect the higher intelligence that we all had now.

It was a different Bible. They didn't use grape juice in tiny, plastic cups once a month during the Lord's Supper. They didn't have a Lottie Moon Christmas Offering. They had wine, and satyrs, and a place with answers. At Delphi, the oracle talked back.

That was the thing.

. . .

Everything was still in order in the 1890s living room. We'd stripped most of the kitchen, the study, the bedroom. Piled what we could of the plank flooring, stacked the loose bricks from the chimney. Round-edged, pink things that were stamped TEXAS. Like the ones in the lot behind the Strip. The ones to be repurposed. The lamented, vigiled bricks.

There was moonlight coming through the windows. Bubbled and creased, like looking through Coke bottles. The Virginia creeper outside the kitchen had grown even farther inside. It obscured the window almost entirely. In places, it had come up through the domino tile. Which we hadn't bothered with. We didn't see much use for tile.

The 1890s half of the house smelled like varnish and tobacco. It had that rich, old huff. Our half smelled like stale glue—and cigarettes, now. The landlord had been saying for two years that he would renovate this half. Rent it out. We didn't want anyone else walking across the foundation, which we would feel on our side.

I turned around when Ruth stepped into the kitchen, an abyss of dark, unfloored pier-and-beam foundation between us.

Had the entrance to Hades been shored up like this? Planked and reinforced? I couldn't remember. What did Orpheus think, walking into the dark? The smoke?

She looked around at the piles. "This is all yours?"

"Ours," I said.

She wrinkled her nose. "Why does it smell like pumpkin?" She was standing next to the window, which looked out over the dark side of the house, where the creepers grew. Where Adam and I had practiced.

I shrugged. "Probably mown grass or something. From earlier."

She tugged at the hem of her baby T-shirt, scrutinizing the place. I thought she looked a bit *hard* for that type of shirt. It was black, at least.

"Why do you have fertilizer?"

She edged around the hole in the floor, toward the creeper.

"Are you . . . *we* going to blow something up?"

I reached out. Gave her a hand around the hole. I didn't want her stepping on the joists. I wasn't sure they were still good.

I looked at the fertilizer. Our Place, where we were going, had already been tilled, used. Fallowed and reused. The fertilizer was for the garden there.

"If we need to."

She stood next to me, looking back at the hollow floor. "How'd you get the fertilizer? Did you buy it?"

"We got it."

"You won't tell me?"

"What does it matter? We bought some things, we stole others. Some we found."

She walked through, trailing a hand over the bricks, over the packets of bamboo seeds on top of the fertilizer. When we first moved in, the landlord sawed down all the bamboo in the back- yard because its stalks spread like weeds. Later, the stumps were hard enough to puncture the wheels on his Jeep when he came back to work on the cross-ties shoring up the parking-lot gravel. We ordered the seeds right after. We'd let them weed all around our Place, to keep wheeled things out. We could use the stalks to fence the gardens. Down deep enough to fuck the prairie dogs and gophers.

She stopped in front of the old bathroom, looking at the dark mirror on the back wall. I'd meant to take the mirror down. To take it with us.

"You read the *Book*?" I asked.

"Yeah," she said. "I don't want a new name."

"You want to be Secondary," I said.

"Yeah."

I didn't say anything. The tattoos on her arm were serpents. Dark mirror, dark hair, dark floor in the darkness. She was nothing like Mary. White Mary with a gun by the Strip.

"I can fix things. Make things."

Bloody Mary.

"Can you weld?"

Bloody Mary.

"A little. Some. I can figure it out."

Bloody Mary.

"All right." I managed a smile. "Until we get there, we'll just call you 'Four.'"

She folded her arms. In the *cold* way, not the *fuck off* way.

"It's better. That we call you something else," I said. "You need to leave what you see with a different name."

"Yeah, I get it."

"You'll still follow orders."

"Yeah."

Orpheus couldn't look back.

I turned, looked back out the front window. I was done talking to her reflection.

"It says that a Place needs a name."

He couldn't look back, or he'd lose her.

"It has a name."

She was quiet for a minute.

In the underworld, nothing ever died. It couldn't. Things lasted forever. Dark places sucked things in: medicines and sports cards from the grocery store, mud, the violence in the parking lot, and the dark outside the Zodiac Arms. The *what the fuck do we do next?* Dark places didn't spit them back out. Nothing came back from Charybdis. The just-a-mouth monster at the bottom of the whirlpool. An ongoing event as being.

Charybdis was a thing that carried meaning across miles and miles and miles. To the sailors in faraway places, through the waves that had the same potential, could be Charybdis anywhere. A Place anywhere.

Our Place was 327 miles away.

"What is it?" she asked.

The ancients even had flowers that lived forever. In the underworld. They thought of everything.

We had read another book. *Native Americans,* which I loved. The Zunis had the same, an immortal flower, continents away from the Greeks. The Zuni rain gods brought it back from the dark. From a different underworld. From different details.

"What is it, Hiram?" she asked.

I didn't remember anything else about the Zunis. Which was fine. I had what I needed.

"It's Amaranth."

"Do you hear that?"

"Where's it coming from?"

I listened. The sound carried easily up through the unfloored pier-and-beam.

"It's from school."

I got down on my knees, looked into the earthy dark, smelling dust.

"It's the bell tower. It uses speakers. Recordings. Fake bells."

I listened again. "Someone's Placed the school."

"What?"

Idiots.

Four pointed over my head, out the window. "Look."

I got up and crept to the window. They were quieter than their own sounds. The sounds of engines and giant, humming tire treads on asphalt finally hit us. A pair of Humvees negotiated the automobile-bramble in the Sycamore intersection. One had a Browning .50-cal mounted on the top. A troop transport followed more sluggishly after.

I felt cold.

"Is that a Group?"

"No. Yes."

Fuck.

"It's the National Guard."

"I thought—"

"Yeah."

THE BOOK:

"TWO"

SEC. "I," SUBSEC. "C," PROCEDURE "I"
("THE FIRST PHASE")

(cont'd)

(v) They should take new names. (vi) They should carry upon them some Mark that identifies their alignment with the Party. (vii) Deliver this Mark in the presence of the rest of the Group, solemnly and with great respect. (viii) This cognitively ordains the Party to its task.

[4] (i) Further, Party Members (and Leaders specifically) should replace terms such as *murder, kill,* or *injure* with *neutralize, remove,* or *incapacitate.* (ii) The Leader should order early acts of violence, rather than leaving their analysis and execution to Party Members, which delivers the Leader from conscience-accountability with the knowledge that he or she did not personally harm a victim. (iii) The Party Member is delivered from such accountability with the knowledge that the voice of the Group directed his or her actions. (iv) The Group is everything. (v) The Party is simply an exploratory idea developing the Narrative. Party Members must be reminded of this often—they are not themselves when in Party.

[5] (i) Leaders and other Party Members must congratulate, thank, or otherwise affirm acts of violence committed by a Party Member in the interest of the operation. (ii) Party Members must be made to feel that their actions are appropriate to the Narrative. (iii) Party Members are encouraged to remember that those they must neutralize or incapacitate are Outsiders—direct opponents to Group survival. (iv) If

Outsiders' survival interests interfere with the Group's, then, morally, these Outsiders are natural enemies—they are predators.

[6] (i) When in Party, look twice, move once. (ii) The obvious strategy is for a Leader to move his or her Party directly into a facility to Forage supplies, counting on martial strength to carry the Party through any necessary violence. This is an unnecessary expenditure of energy, as well as an unnecessary risk. (iii) Party excursions are conservative operations. (iv) Remember that, while it is unseen and generally unknowable, personal energy is a Group's greatest resource. It must be replenished with food, water, and rest, all of which will be in precious supply. (v) As such, squandering energy with unnecessary maneuvers or unnecessary risk is a crime of waste, committed against the Group.

CHAPTER EIGHT

Should I wake them up?" Four whispered.

"No." I waved absently at the front wall, trying to set the black-and-white's earpiece in place with my other hand. It was a leftover, a yellowed plastic thing that had come with the crystal radio kit my dad and I bought. We had built it together when I was twelve. The year I'd quit the Boy Scouts. It had been something we'd done together—he was one of the Assistant Scout Masters. They all were—one assistant for each Scout, fathers all, even if that made for a clumsy Administration. When I quit, he was commuting back and forth, from Dallas to Little Rock, because he'd lost his old job. Arkansas during the week, Texas on the weekends—when we did things like launch model rockets and build crystal radios. The Scouts had been ours, not mine, so I didn't go because he couldn't go. I went back when he did.

That was the first time we ceased to be a family.

The earpiece fit the black-and-white's audio jack better than our other earphones.

"Just keep watch," I told her.

The black-and-white's dials were very small. Levi and I had to be careful with them because, over time, my dad had stripped many of the tiny, plastic teeth from the housing that cinched the dial onto the much-thinner tuning rod. We had to press and turn at the same time, or the dials would just spin.

My heartbeat was coming to a late realization about what Four and I had just seen. About what it meant. It started working itself up. I spun the dials a few times, ineffectually, forgetting to *Depress the clutch, or you'll kill it*. I clenched my teeth to keep from cursing. Calmed down.

KHED was one of our favorite 'casts, even though he didn't use video often. I didn't want to hunt for anything new. As I turned the dial through the frequencies, I heard a lot of static. Several of the 'casts weren't active anymore.

Salvage was thinning out.

I found KHED. It was a simple 'cast—just the digital newscasts, stripped out of their feed (video, too, this time) and re-'cast, ana-log, for Salvage. I wondered how many people, other than KHED, could even still see the original report. Without power. Who out-side of Salvage would have any idea that things had escalated? To the point that KHED wasn't fucking with the feed. To the point that no jammers were fucking with him not fucking with the feed.

I took my hands off the dials and grabbed the stenographer's pad. Shoved the earpiece in deeper. I tried to be dutiful about this. The news anchor was trying to sound objective. The most important thing was keeping a clear perspective on the Collapse, though she didn't call it that. They—digital, everyone else—didn't have a name for it.

I took notes of images and feeds in case they showed up in somebody's 'cast later. I didn't know how much longer we'd be in Slade, but it would be better to know what Salvage was reusing, from where, just in case:

• *Trouble at many major universities.*
Clashes between law enforcement and National Guard personnel and anarchist demonstrators, who call themselves "Salvage." Casualties on both sides. Law enforcement suffering from record numbers of MIA or AWOL personnel.

(video feed: burning university buildings, Humvees, Salvage weapons fire, law enforcement nerve-agent clouds.)

Our school was shown, briefly, in the unrest slideshow. Nothing was burning yet, and no one seemed to be firing, but there were Groups, or Parties (I couldn't tell), on the campus, and they looked, in that brief moment, like they might be mobilizing. We'd already seen the fucking Humvees outside.

• *Churches being burned, bombed, attacked by armed gangs.*

(video feed: burning steeples, smoke-belching windows, stained glass glowing from the inside. People.)

I knew what this was about. The churches in the cities—the mosques and temples, the tabernacles and worship centers, the ones with ribbons of fleeing refugees like licking tongues streaming from the double doors to the streets outside—those would be gang attacks. The ones in the urban centers. Attacked from each corner, from streets with saints' names.

But those streets were no longer divine. Their builders had offered them up, sacrificed Any Other Name, to be sure their cities paid tribute to God's favorites. Now the streets were just lines, marking ganglands. There was nothing special about these churches. There were no secret histories or clandestine reliquaries. No one named pillars anymore, or stored sacred things in hollow places. Paid attention to divine blueprints, or built mysteries around their architects. These days, Solomon and David were an LLP—a firm downtown, perhaps, that had done civil buildings and art museums. One of the companies that designed churches, that also did movie theaters, schools, prisons. Because the schematics were the same, handed all the way down from the Second Temple: how to contain people according to God's will.

Now they were just places to gather. Interchangeable. Forgettable. Flammable.

Any gang leader knew he had to get the jump if he was going to come out on top in all of this. Or stay on top. He had to carve out the new holy places. Thin them out. Place the holiest of holies somewhere in *his* territory.

The other churches, though—the empty ones, burning just the same—those would be Salvage attacks cutting out the risk before it could take root. Southern Salvage was terrified of churches. People would get scared, so they'd go to church. They'd eat church food, pray church prayers. Then they'd get hungry: a bunch of scared, well-armed southerners. In massive mobs. Not Groups. Who all believed they were right by God.

It wouldn't take long, Chance had figured, before they'd start trying to spread the Good News at the ends of their rifles. Soon it would be God's Will to survive, to be fruitful and multiply, and the Outsiders were threats. Nephilim. The Canaanites in the way. The mechanics of staying alive would rewrite the rules, and the South would be dotted with well-armed city-state theocracies. Military councils in Family Life Centers. Exercise on the old playgrounds. Procreation and Programming in the Nursery.

It would be a nightmare. I didn't care much. With the Na-

tional Guard and the police firing at them, though, Salvage was
going to care less and less about making sure to go after only
empty buildings and disabling facilities, resources, or threats in
benign, nonviolent ways.

> In a joint operation with the FBI, ATF agents in Georgia
> clashed with a terrorist organization called "Fat Chance"
> in a religious separatist compound near the city of
> Macon. The group was identified by the FBI as a key
> element in a nationwide epidemic of anti-State activity.
> Over fifty separatists are reported dead.

I stopped. Chance had never been in New York.

I looked at the reporting bitch who gave the news.

It was a diversion, I realized. Up the seaboard, because the rest
of Salvage had become *too* interested in the Chance. In its whereabouts, maybe. It was smart. They weren't taking any chances.

I looked at the note.

Terrorist organization.

Religious.

Compound.

I listened. They killed them. Killed Fat Chance and Slim
Chance, Slow Moses, the Jeté. White. All of them.

> Authorities traced the group through a federal fraud in-
> vestigation. The group reportedly channeled funds and
> resources through unlicensed religious revival broad-
> casts, which they aired on a number of Citizens' Televi-
> sion Band frequencies outside FCC regulation. The
> group, which relied upon CTB enthusiasts to help
> spread its messages, operated as "The Redemption
> Network," raising over one million dollars for its cause.

It was praised for its reactionary conservatism by a number of prominent conservative PACs and pro-values organizations.

But White had just started the story—"The Last Man"—with her last 'cast. How the hell would we get the rest of it? Crack its code?

If this was real—if Chance had laundered that money . . .

I made myself write another note.

As word first spread of confrontation with the Fat Chance terrorist organization, underground anarchists nationwide responded with demonstrations, attacks, and acts of civil disorder. Other religious separatist groups have reportedly launched attacks against domestic defense and law enforcement forces.

. . . then they took their . . . *infantile steps criminally. . . .*

The Plan *was supposed to be a reaction—not a catalyst, not a revolution.*

I wanted to hit the news anchor. "Anarchist." I wanted to hit her. She didn't know what it meant.

. . . *Pre-Event, take the time to learn the whereabouts of nearby paramilitary Groups, which may include religious or philosophical sects, racial supremacists, or other paralegal organizations. Avoid routes that will take your Group past these Places. . . .*

Chance's 'casting campaign had been preemptive. Spreading the Good Word about the dangers of churches. In the South. Chance had mobilized the rest of Salvage—it got everyone to Clear its competitors. Tricked other Salvagers into avoiding the roads that would lead others to Chance's Promised Land. Which was real, though: Chance or Redemption?

Had we been complicit? Or was this bullshit? Of course we weren't our-fucking-selves when in Party. Not if we were fulfilling someone else's Plan—Chance's Plan—without fucking knowing it.

The generators in the Hoover Dam have been compromised, as a part of this increasing wave of domestic terrorist attacks. Large portions of the southwestern US are now without power.

We'd be just as clueless as all these Outsiders, *Book*s or not.

I pulled the earpiece out. Four turned and looked at me.

"Any more Guard?" I asked.

"No."

"Wake them up." I handed her the stenographer's pad. "Give Levi the report. Do it calmly. Don't wake them in a panic."

"Where are you going?"

"Just outside. A check."

I picked up one of the walkie-talkies and the .38. I was careful, slipping out the back door. Anyone could be waiting among the palisades of bamboo obscuring the fence. I moved slowly, across the gravel lot, through the stalks, toward the fence. *We taught ourselves ninjutsu and tried it out in the fort. In the field between us and the grocery store.* Against the fence, I could hear the bell tower better, but I still couldn't tell what they were saying.

They'd taken the campus for White. For Fat Chance.

I tuned the walkie-talkie to Channel 19. The Salvage Channel. The most popular, anyway. What came through matched the mumbled bell tower broadcast in cadence. Someone was standing close enough to pick up what was coming from those hidden speakers. Close enough to give it to the rest of Slade. 'Casters would piggyback it. Take it from their own walkie-talkies, and pump it straight into their amps, into their modded antennae. Word would spread.

I listened.

Last made his goggles with cobalt-blue Depression bottles. He filed the shattered bases smooth and secured them over his ears with wire. He printed a trowel inside the shanty—

It was White's voice, cut off. Probably the last portion to make it out of New York. Out of Georgia. Chance must've been real. It had to be.

Somebody local had gotten the last portion. Whoever it was, they weren't 'casting the story like they were supposed to. They were asserting it. Moving it from the Salvage airwaves to something physical. Speaking into a microphone atop the bell tower, or jacking a portable data player into whatever mixing deck controlled the volume, the pitch, the timbre of the school's artificial bells. Whoever this was, they were creating an oracle. A call to prayer. You had to come out of the dark places, out of Salvage-hiding to listen to the rest of the story.

And they'd been cut off. I didn't hear any weapons fire. Even at this distance, I'd hear it if they'd shelled the tower.

A sniper, though, could have done it quietly. Silenced the speakers, severed the nerve thinking the mob.

Except, if I was right—if those were Cells or Groups on campus—there wasn't a nerve to sever. Just Phantom Cell Structure. It wasn't a mob. It was the confluence of different Places, all thinking across their distances. Shooting one kid in a tower or destroying the device playing the story into the speakers wouldn't demoralize the Salvage on campus. It would light it on fire. It would make the campus into all Places at once. It would make it a terrain that looked different, looked safe in different ways to everyone with something to throw or shoot at the Guard.

. . . *When you reach your Place, consider it enemy territory.* . . .

Now was our chance. The government had accelerated things. It wasn't supposed to be this unstable for weeks. The country was starting to burn. I'd guess the whole world was starting to burn.

Now was our chance. We needed to get the jump. We were going to need more than just the four of us. To be strong.

We needed the rest of White's story.

"Because we need the rest of the story," I said. "We need some fucking answers."

Four was being calm. I'd told Levi and Mary about Four. She was asking sound questions, which was good. We hadn't assigned a Party Leader yet, so asking questions was still good.

"You don't understand," Levi said.

"White's story, 'The Last Man,' is going to be a part of Salvage."

"Whatever it'll be like now," Mary said.

I looked at her. "Yeah."

"We're going to need the rest of that story," I said. "It'll be a stock in trade. It'll be a thing between Salvagers."

"Do you even know what it means?"

"It's just a story," I said.

"It's a story about survival," Levi said. "It's a metaphor. A code."

"Like the crib sheets?"

"Yes."

"It's not just about 'survival,'" Mary said. "It's about 'self,' too." She tied her bandanna over her head. It would be under her mask.

"'The Last Man,'" Four said. "It's a religion. You're chasing after your own grail."

I smirked. She didn't get it. "It isn't a religion."

"It's *about* a Group with one brain, *from* a Group with one brain. One brain to rule them all," she said.

She didn't get it.

Mary reached for the polish, for her face. Levi stayed her hand. There wasn't a Party yet. No Leader meant no paint.

"No one *believes* in the Last Man," I said. "He doesn't *get* you anything. No heavens, no blessings, no bread from the sky. It's just a story."

"About being last," Levi said.

"That's what a religion is," Four said. She took the can of polish from Levi. "The perfect, final, static self. I read the *Book*. I get it. It's fine. We're going after the new religion. That's fine. We're going after some others, who don't know yet what they're going after. After some answers."

I looked at her. She was ready to paint Mary white. She was holding the can so she could paint Mary with her other hand.

"That's fine," Four said. "We should all go. This is important."

"I think Hiram should Lead the Party," Four said.

"You Lead, Hiram?" Levi asked.

They all looked at me.

. . . *You are not yourselves.* . . .

She doesn't get it.

"I'll Lead."

Ruth started painting Mary. "I need a mask."

Levi and I exchanged looks.

"I thought you wanted to be Secondary."

"Yes."

"You want in on this?" I asked. "You want a mask?"

She closed Mary's eyelids, gently. "I have to have *something*."

THE BOOK:

"TWO"

SEC. "I," SUBSEC. "C," PROCEDURE "I" ("THE FIRST PHASE")

(cont'd)

[7] (i) It is better for the Party to use the energy of others to its advantage. (ii) The key to the First Phase of the Event Exit Strategy is to execute the maneuver before too much time passes. (iii) In the early period following the Event, when civil unrest outpaces law enforcement, great numbers of urban Outsiders will flock to places such as grocery stores, pharmacies, feed suppliers, and hardware stores. (iv) Some will waste their energy at electronics stores and other commodity suppliers. Avoid these facilities.

[8] (i) The Party is watching for disorder. (ii) The most conservative Forage occurs outside facilities wherein chaos reigns. The reason behind this is that the situation offers the greatest capitalization on the personal energies of others. (iii) Those that do successfully negotiate internal facility disorder will have expended great amounts of personal energy in doing so (indeed, they may already have sustained injuries), which makes them ideal targets.

[9] (i) The maneuver does not begin until you have established surveillance. (ii) The surveillance officer's primary duty is to watch for signs of risk—approaching mobs, rogue military patrols, or competing Parties endanger your Party, necessitating abortion and reassignment.

[10] (i) In the theater of violence itself is the acquisitions team. (ii) Ideally, they are three. (iii) If your Party has only three Members, then the surveillance operation must

necessarily be rolled into their tasks. (iv) Under these circumstances, the tolerance for risk is higher, for the Party must acquire the supplies it needs, risk or not.

[11] (i) The most conservative form of the maneuver involves three roles for the acquisitions team: diplomat, mule, and escort. (ii) The diplomat approaches Outsiders as they exit the facility, having successfully negotiated the disorder inside. (iii) The diplomat requests the supplies in question from the target. (iv) If the target declines, the diplomat threatens force. (v) If the target reciprocates, the three incapacitate the target and Forage the supplies. (vi) The mule moves the Foraged goods out of the immediate theater and into a nearby cache. (vii) The escort monitors surrounding activity and will defend the mule and his or her payload, should either come to risk. (viii) The Party must remember that its behavior is not its own. (ix) You are not yourselves. (x) The Place is thinking, and it requires vicious behavior.

[12] (i) Repeat this process until it becomes infeasible.

CHAPTER NINE

I wasn't Senior Patrol Leader then. I think I might have been Assistant Patrol Leader. I might have just been in a patrol. I can't remember.

We were lost. Doing our duty to God and our country. Remembering the Boy Scout Law. Being Prepared. But we were on the wrong trail. Our dads had gone ahead, driving the pickup trucks and vans and SUVs to the campsite off the state park road. They had set up their camp, percolated coffee over the fire in blue-enameled steel pots. Sat in camp chairs in Boy Scout cargo shorts. They wore their socks up to their shins. It was regulation. They were setting good examples.

There were twenty-three of us, and we each carried a compass. There was only one map, however. One SPL, two Assistant SPLs, four Patrol Leaders, four Assistant Patrol Leaders. I was one of these, somewhere in the ranks, one of the youngest in the troop. I'd been allowed in early because of my Arrow of Light. Earning the Arrow of Light, in the Webelos, got you in early. Got you the training earlier than others.

We had aluminum-frame packs, hiking boots, Sierra cups on

our belts. Pocketknives, waterproof matches, flashlights with belt clips and buttons for signaling in Morse code. We had all these things lost with us, standing in a mob on the hiking trail. We were earning our Orienteering Merit Badges, arguing directions beneath black oaks. Among creepers and ferns and tiny signs identifying other plants.

The SPL's name was an anagram. All things were anagrams, some without vowels. I'd learned this from the back-page puzzles in *Boys' Life* magazine. A subscription came with your dues to the troop, and it told stories of loyalty, Christianity, and service. The magazines featured pictures of concept cars and kits for turning vacuums into hovercrafts. There were ads for throwing-knife targets, for air rifles, for gun camps. There were articles on how to make bridges out of rope.

I didn't speak into the mob. Into the noise. Everyone else was older than me. We were tired. We were lost. One of the boys was crying. I couldn't do orienteering. Not well. I could do fires. I won awards for starting fires with wet wood, for starting them at competitions in artificial winds blown from rented industrial fans.

I stuck with what I knew. I learned how to make all kinds of fires all kinds of ways. To do my duty to God and my Country.

We were walking to the square. That was something. I didn't want to chance the Mulberry Mob again, though they'd likely dispersed when the Guard rolled through. Those that Mary hadn't burned. The Oak Street intersection wasn't much farther down Broadway. We stayed away from the road, moving when we could through office buildings and parking garages. I didn't want to chance the truck, or the car. There was too high a chance that we wouldn't have open roads. We'd be an obvious target, and if we hit a roadblock, we didn't have the artillery to get ourselves out.

Four had helped Levi rig some more cocktails, with motor oil and gas from a can that we used to fill the lawn mower. We carried two each, on lariats I'd tied for the purpose. Four carried six. She would replace what we used. I assigned the .38 to Mary because she couldn't use a sword.

Later, when I was SPL, when everyone was younger than me, after the troop's first Eagle Scout had gone to prison, after the second had joined the police force, I told them that we weren't lost. There wasn't any discussion. I allowed only Patrol Leaders to carry compasses. Everyone had jobs. Orient, read. Carry the matches. Be important to the troop. *We need you to do this.* I had my Assistant SPLs run checks, talk with Patrol Leaders about fatigue, morale, backaches. I called stops for rest before the others had to ask. They voted me into the Order of the Arrow for this, and I spent a weekend without talking, among other Order initiates, sleeping on the ground without a tent. I kept the secrets from the rest of the troop. Like I was supposed to. When someone cried, I put him in charge of something. Made him responsible to something other than being twelve years old and tired. Made him somebody. Promised him I'd show him how to make fire. I'd call him Prometheus, like calling him "Sport." I'd learned it at his age, reading *Mythology*. They didn't know what it meant, but they liked taking a new name.

On Oak Street, we moved in Z-file, staggered. Mary followed me, Four followed her. Levi walked last. Without streetlights, without flashlights and campfires, we could see the stars. The blurry band of the Milky Way. On Scout campouts, we couldn't even see any constellations—they were too polluted by their own stars, and our dads had to bend the rules to get us our Astronomy Merit Badges, out west at summer camp.

Even Mary, in her white, was hard to see in the dark when I turned around. I led them straight down the center of the road, between parked and abandoned cars. I wouldn't take them right up against the historic homes that lined the street because I didn't want to alarm anyone. I didn't want to give anyone a reason to think we had come for their things.

At one house, we heard people talking in the side yard, behind a fence. Male voices.

. . . Take no chances. . . .

I stopped us. Pulled us into a crouching cluster in the middle of the road.

"Mary," I ordered. "Cocktail."

I couldn't let this bunch, talking into the dark, get the jump on us.

She pulled loose a cocktail and set it on the asphalt. Four handed her another to fill the empty lariat.

"Light it," I told Four.

She did, hiding the mostly blue flame with her cupped hands.

"Levi," *Prometheus,* "divert their attention."

I looked at Mary. Grabbed her shoulder. "You and Four, thirty yards ahead. Get the jump."

She grabbed Four, and they took off, sprinting low and quiet. Practicing ninjutsu without the tall grass. You were supposed to run like your hands were holding rails.

I stood up with Levi, and he threw the cocktail.

• • •

On my twenty-first birthday, Adam and I went bar-hopping around the Strip. On the way home, down Oak Street, with its better sidewalks than Mulberry, I bummed cigarette after cigarette from Adam. I'd been smoking them with him that night, which was something new to do—together—since returning from the West. From the university in Lubbock, that first year. From weekend visits to my cousin's farm.

Later, I convinced him to quit.

The Strip-rat was not in the street anymore. When I looked at the Wailing Wall, I was tired. It showed something that couldn't have been real, so I looked away. It was dark.

It couldn't have been real.

I didn't look back, in case it was.

Around two corners, a few blocks away, someone was shouting into a bullhorn. They'd be on Meyer Street, which once contained the fronts of the Strip, before the renovation began. Nearby, there'd be the three-story Auditorium Building at the edge of campus. One of many massive buildings with cement walls behind brick walls between wet walls. We took our literature classes there, listening to musicians practice on the massive, one-of-a-kind organ in the heart of the building. In the auditorium that was no longer used.

We'd scoped the building before. If you boarded up the glass windows, it'd be impenetrable. The Guard wouldn't be able to take it except by siege if Salvage had holed up inside. There would be massive casualties on both sides, particularly for the invaders.

The building had a basement, with a crawl space. You could use it to gain access to the municipal sewer line under Meyer. We had the specs.

"In the event of a separation," I said to the Party, "rendezvous in the Oak Street Building. In the courtyard."

I took ceramics classes in the Oak Street Building. It was behind us, over our shoulders really, a satellite just off the main campus.

They nodded.

"If you wait there, alone, for over an hour, fall back to the HOC."

Gunfire erupted. I heard the pneumatic grunts of nerve-agent cannons. It would be mild stuff, with a narrow radius.

That *thing*, on the Wall, couldn't have been real. There was nothing wrong with us. With the *Book*.

The storefront windows went all at once, concussed from their frames. Books fell off the shelves easily. Between semesters, the university bookstore didn't keep as many, so the shelves were lightly packed. You only had so long to sell your texts back before the next semester. They sent them back and then bought them again. Over and over, emptying and filling shelves. It wasn't owned by the university, but you had to buy your books there.

We learned that "Used Saves."

The Party was fine, in the middle of the store, against one wall. I checked.

There'd been a kid with a gun standing by the front window. The Meyer Street window. Now he had glass in his face. In his eyes. There was a piece lodged in his throat, an alien flap silencing his screams. He was horribly alive.

I took his .30-caliber Beretta, the ammo. A crib sheet from his back pocket. He had a hypodermic needle. If he was Salvage, on recon, or a recruiter, maybe, it was his ticket out. The chemical

stylus that would shear the layers of his brain, wiping him out
and the intel he had with him.

I shoved it in his neck and depressed the plunger. Because in the
Boy Scouts, you take an oath to "Help other people at all times."

If it was morphine, or something like, he'd die shitfaced and
weightless.

Be prepared, our fathers had taught us.

Outside, in the middle of Meyer, one of the Humvees was a
burning shell. The blast had blown the wheels off, which meant
it had come from underneath. There was a hole in the asphalt
under the truck. Someone had moved through the crawl space
under the Auditorium Building and blown the shit out of the
Guard. The smoke looked like a hydra, streaming out from
under the Humvee in cohesive pillars. It smelled like smoke and
sulfur. The brimstone from the underground sewer.

Demolitions cooks were usually Secondary Party Members.
Somebody had cooked the shit out of something before they
stuck it under that Humvee.

I thought about Four, staring at the mirror, dark snakes in
the darkness. We had given her a black mask, and she wore black
paint, like us.

If the kid on the floor had been wearing a mask, the glass had
torn it away.

A different Humvee, farther up Meyer, opened fire on the
Auditorium Building. There was a Guard in a riot mask firing
the .50-caliber machine gun from the top of the truck's frame.

I saw two other Guards standing behind the Humvee, loading
a rocket-propelled grenade launcher—an RPG, which was the
same acronym we used for "role-playing game." For D&D.

I stepped away from the kid.

• • •

They'd retreated to the store's office, on my orders.

"We're going to need the assault Humvee," I told Levi.

"Why?"

I looked at him. I thought about that image on the Wailing Wall. It couldn't have been real. I had nothing to worry about.

But if it wasn't, what else hadn't been real?

There would be nothing more from Fat Chance. White would never be Hope again. The Last Man was fucked from the get-go. After all, *last* implies the slow and eventual removal. Of everybody. Otherwise, he'd just be called "The Man."

If it was real, then it wasn't going to go that way. Not if I could get that Humvee. Not if I had that .50-cal, and that RPG, and those nerve agents. If I had them, I could make them burn—anybody who wanted to make that message real.

"No questions. Not in Party."

He remembered. Nodded.

"What's the complement?" he asked.

I told him.

"Armament?"

I told him.

I looked down. "Who's this corpse?"

In the back of the office, there were others, still alive. Mary was on her knees, writing something down—something one of them was saying. There were about ten of them. They looked scared. They were looking at Mary. At White Mary. At a new Hope.

Four was kneeling against the other wall, whispering into one's ear. A girl. She had her hands on the girl's shoulders. The girl was nodding.

"The corpse took a forty-four blast to the spine," Levi said, "from the one with Four."

I looked at Four's girl.

"The corpse made a go at Mary when she stepped in to secure the room. The girl with the forty-four over there knew what the corpse was up to. Perfect angle. Knew the Plan. Overtake the Outsiders, I'm guessing."

"Didn't seem to like the idea," I said.

I looked again at Mary. She had untied her mask. Four had painted her entire face and neck white before we left. She looked porcelain, a doll. The virgin queen.

I smirked. "Four's girl saw a pure, white Mary step into the darkness."

"White Mary."

"She liked that Plan better."

"They're one Party, but different Groups."

"What?"

Levi turned back to look at them. "It was a coordinated operation—some of the best cooks around, sent to task by their Leaders."

Organized Salvage?

"The hell?"

"They aren't Primary. Were only here to wait on their escort out."

Jesus. The kid with the syringe had been their sentry.

"Leaders wouldn't risk them running around town on their own."

"Where's the escort?" I asked.

"An hour late."

I turned to leave. "Line them up."

"Where are you going?"

"Stop asking questions."

• • •

Mary was standing next to me. They'd lined them up.

"Did you get the last line of White's story? From one of them?"

"Yes."

"Read it."

Last made his goggles with cobalt-blue Depression bottles. He filed the shattered bases smooth and wore them with wire. He printed a trowel inside the shanty . . .

Mary looked at me. That was where it had cut off—where our version of the story had originally ended.

"Read the rest."

. . . and ground his spare glass into the earth. The water it made gave him the mud. Last worked in the sun. Last made bricks to build walls for his dead.

"How many Groups are you?" I asked the line. Eight male, two female—

I was fifteen the first time I created a secret society. With Chuck and Adam. We created a knighthood.

—Mary looked at me. I nodded.

"This isn't an interrogation," she said.

"We don't want your Groups' intel. Just the details of this operation."

By-laws. Codes of conduct. An entire philosophy for secret life. Salvage had rites and contests and ways for determining Leadership.

"Six," Four's girl said.

Six. Christ.

"Who's Party Leader, then?" I asked.

A couple of them looked at each other. Most were looking at Mary.

"Gong," one said. "The sentry by the Meyer door."

"Dead," I told them.

"We had a rendezvous point here, in the bookstore," Four's girl said. "It was planned once White's last broadcast came through."

She looked down at her hands. "They were going to get us out. Take us back"—

In our knighthood, we wore key rings on chains around our necks. A circle, our symbol. We wore them at all times. I wore mine that summer, on an exchange trip. Italy, Austria, Hungary. Trying to live with honor in foreign countries.

—"What happened?"

"We don't know."

"You're cooks," I said. "All of you?"

"Yes"—

In the order, in the knighthood, we had new names. Titles and epithets. Designations of rank.

—"You cooked the trap under the Humvee?"

"Yes."

"But your Leaders wouldn't let you detonate it."

"Too much risk, they said," one of the males said. "Even running like fuck, through the service tunnels under the road."

"Your escort is probably up to its ass in artillery, on campus."

"You can't stay here," Mary said.

"Are you staying with your families?" Four asked.

"Don't ask about their families."

"Ishmael was supposed to come," Four's girl said.

I looked at Levi.

• • •

"Mary, talk to them. Find out."

I signaled Levi: *Make the offer.*

I walked away. To do Something Important, as far as they were concerned.

I came back.

"Dietary restrictions?" I asked Mary.

"No."

"Medical?"

"No."

One of the cooks had worked the grenade-launcher mod for his 20-gauge. He had at least ten shells and dowel mounts around his waist, under his belt. But he didn't have any cocktails. Levi and I had thought about the modification before, but we didn't have shotguns.

We had plenty of cocktails.

I handed Four a pile of T-shirts, all the same color. Red was all I could find—it was the school color. Levi gave Mary tubes of paint from the school spirit section, also red. They were for painting your face—for football games.

The first kid stood still. Rigid.

I pushed the cap off a black marker. I didn't have any other way of doing this. On his left cheekbone, I drew a wildstyle A and one down-pointing chevron beneath. Mary painted around it. Ruth cut the shirts for their masks. They would look like Imperial Guard, I realized—

When it's your turn, when it's you in the Boy Scouts, inducting initiates, giving them the secrets of the Order of the Arrow, you don't have to keep quiet. It's your job to listen for discussion. You cut chips in their arrows—the ones the inductees have carved and wear on lariats around their necks—when they speak. You tell them secrets, Indian stories, and make them work.

—I went down the line.

"Your first-place is the House of Cards."

They were well armed. Each of them. Outfitted like Primaries. Probably the best their Groups could give them.

"Our objective is the Humvee firing on the Auditorium Building, and the equipment carried by its Guard. This will be, primarily, an exercise in vigilance."

They liked being told what to do. They weren't in the corners anymore. They had White Mary now. A mother and a whore, carrying a gun. It was the hyperbolic Freudian dream, and she was wearing the paint for the role.

"The Group is everything. If Outsiders' survival interests interfere with the Group's, then, morally, these Outsiders are natural enemies. They are predators."

I finished the last one and stepped back. Let Mary and Four work their way down the line.

"You do not have names. You will take new names. For now, until we've reached the HOC, you will be referred to as Jacks. You will follow orders. At the HOC, we will give you a new *Book*."

I waved Levi forward.

"We will take you to a Place," he said, "where we will be safe—where we will be strong."

If I can get the fire from the Humvee.

I looked at him for a long time.

To make them burn.

The thing about wildstyle graffiti is that no one writes it the same way. No one wrote A's just the way I did, or used chevrons underneath.

But it was *my* tag on the Wall.

I'd never tagged anything.

So it couldn't have been real—

We had disbanded the knighthood one year later because we wanted to kill it before we stopped believing it was real.

—"You are not yourselves," I said. I looked away, toward Mary. I wanted her to cinch this.

"Mary, divide them up. Two Parties. Secure this building.

"Four, get that grenade launcher armed.

"Levi, get some graph paper."

THE BOOK:

"TWO"

SEC. "I," SUBSEC. "C," PROCEDURE "II"
("THE SECOND PHASE")

[1] (i) The Second Phase assumes the successful execution of the First. (ii) It assumes the Group has reconvened in toto at the first-place, Party casualties notwithstanding. (iii) If the First Phase is forgone, proceed directly to the Second Phase, the Evacuation.

[2] (i) You may Evacuate by a number of different means.

> (a) (i) If one of your Members is a qualified pilot, travel by air; however, be prepared to Forage wheeled vehicles from the areas around your Place after you Arrive—you will need them during later Place operations.

> (b) (i) Rely on trains only if you must and only if one of your Members can operate a locomotive. (ii) Trains' dependence upon their tracks makes them vulnerable.

> (c) (i) If you must reach your Place via boat, rely on smaller, faster craft—use several if you can. (ii) When traveling by water, keep other craft at a distance—if they draw near, disable them, either by weapons fire or by the use of incendiary devices. (iii) Risk tolerance approaches zero when traveling via watercraft.

> (d) (i) Evacuating by car, truck, or diesel transport is your most likely method. (ii) Take the time to secure fuel. (iii) Do not secure all of your supplies or fuel in one vehicle. (iv) Use at least enough vehicles that if one is compromised, its crew, supplies, and passengers can be adequately transferred to the other vehicles. (v)

Off-road-capable trucks are advised. (vi) Where
possible, avoid the use of highways and other roads.
(vii) Avoid traveling through urban centers at
absolutely all cost.

[3] (i) When the terrain requires you to travel by road, organized
shipping lane, or established flight path, attempt to keep an
Outsider's vehicle in sight at all times. (ii) You may need to
disable this other vehicle in order to Forage parts, should
one of yours require repair. (iii) When possible, avoid
"roadside" repairs and simply confiscate other vehicles. (iv)
Expect resistance.

[4] (i) Your vehicles should not drive so closely together upon the
open roads that they would be disabled simultaneously by
anti-vehicle fire, roadside bombs, or other devices. (ii) If one
vehicle is compromised, the other(s) should travel far
enough ahead to double back and safely neutralize the
roadside threat before attempting a rescue.

CHAPTER TEN

they took their paint off, Mary and Four. Used some blood from the corpse in the office to distress their shirts. They ran tangentially toward the Humvee, so they wouldn't surprise the Guard. Mary had her gun tucked under her waistband, up against her ass.

The Guard didn't shoot the girls when they ran—panicking, yelling, bloodied, and wide-eyed—toward them. For help. For sanctuary. Five of the Jacks were watching from the roof, from the corner nearest the Humvee—Aleph Party. There was definitely another firefight deeper into campus, they reported. Around the bell tower.

Two of the other Jacks were at the far corner, looking the other way down Meyer. We'd given one, the leader, my walkie-talkie. He would coordinate between his Party, Beta, and the last Party, Chi, who were at the other end of the roof, watching over Oak Street. He reported to Levi, whom I put in charge of the operation. To call it off, to redirect as needed. I was the free agent. I wanted it that way, for this. The Jacks would see Mary, their bloodied Mary, take the risk. Get things moving.

They needed to see one of us seal the deal—me or Levi. See us save her and take what we needed. She was their Mary, had been so from that first white moment, bringing light to the darkness in the office, where they had been abandoned.

One of the Guards, the one with the nerve-agent cannon, sent two canisters at the Auditorium Building, their basso grunts like hooting owls as their ejecta smokestreamed toward the building. As I'd thought, the agent clouds were cohesive. They vented up into the opened windows, before the wind dispersed them, on the second and third floors, through which Salvage was firing. The break in the firefight bought the Guard a minute to address the girls.

Aleph Party, on Levi's command, fired the grenade launcher over the Humvee toward the building, between the Guard and Salvage, to divert their attention.

We had to hurry. There might have been another demolitions squad worming through the underground. The Jacks had made enough for several vehicles, but they didn't know how much would be used. If there was another squad, they'd blow a new hole in the road, taking people down into the darkness to live dead forever with flowers that wouldn't die. Zunis and Greeks and kids from Slade, trading all the final answers with the oracle. Giving them back, maybe, at Delphi. Asynchronously. Offering answers from the future, when things Collapsed, to the classical ancients waiting patiently to be as intelligent as we were, at twelve years old, in our seventh-grade classroom, reading *Mythology* and *Native Americans*.

The answers hadn't made sense to the ancients because they'd been for us, in the future. They just built meaning from the abstracta. It was a trick psychics used.

Mary was ready. She got the jump. She shot one Guard through the back of the neck when he turned around to flinch at Aleph Party's exploding cocktail. When he turned around *to help other people at all times.*

If I could, I would have just made them the offer. To give us what we want, or die. But they would have just killed us. We could . . . *take no chances. . . .*

Four grabbed the other Guard's gun, the one who loaded the RPG and the nerve-agent cannon, just so he couldn't use it. She wasn't hurting him, which was Secondary.

The driver slid out of his cockpit, taking a moment to help while Salvage battled the gas in the building. When he turned to shoot Four, to shoot Mary, I ran through the burning-Humvee-smoke-hydra. I emerged from underground, wearing goggles and a respirator from the art section in the bookstore. I wore all-black, was painted black, to be part of the smoke, the power-outage darkness. I was not myself in the tall grass outside the fort.

On the roof, everyone had become Primary. The Jacks opened fire on the gunner in the back of the Humvee. I opened fire on the driver. When Four let go, Mary opened fire on the other Guard. We all brought fire, unbound. Prometheus, every one.

It was a tight fit, the four of us and one Jack in the Humvee. The other Jacks had trucks in the parking lot on the Oak Street side of the bookstore. They had shells over the beds. They had a half-assed mobile lab, which they had used to finish priming the explosives once they were on site.

They looked too young for this. Eighteen, tops.

"Did you have another rendezvous point? A Place for falling back?" I asked our Jack. "Where your Primaries would have gone when they split?"

"No," he said, flushed and breathing firm. Safe and confident in here with us. "It was just back to our Place. Our Group's Place. It was agreed on by the Leaders."

We were going to need the rest of their equipment, their full labs. Their Primaries were probably just as young as these.

I drove the Humvee away from the Auditorium Building, up Meyer. It made sense. Now Salvage could come together in the heart of campus, to do away with whoever, whatever, had killed White's last words. But not us. We had the last words, were strong now. I wouldn't throw resources away on a fight that didn't even need us.

Now, with the Humvee, I had what I needed to make sure it didn't become real. We were strong now. No one would end up alone. It was just more noise.

There was nothing wrong with the *Book*.

Levi turned around. "What you did was right."

In the streets around us, on the way back, people were organizing. Not Salvage, just people with flashlights and baseball bats. Guns. Neighbors and families forming posses.

Already.

They stared, standing in their front yards and along their sidewalks, as I threaded the caravan down Meyer. The street was tight here, where tract houses closed in on one another. The trees lining the road had formed a tunnel of leaves and branches that blocked out the sky.

Levi jumped channels on his walkie-talkie—he was monitoring the Salvage bands as we took the long way back, which would take us past another electrical substation, along a longhorn pasture, and eventually back to Broadway.

"It's the Lull," he said, looking up. "Most of the civil responders are on the north side of town."

"How big's the response?"

These weren't Salvage people. They weren't organizing, they were congregating, tightening the suburban herd against the predators in the tall grass. Which meant that the violence and the vandalism and the initial terror had subsided enough that they'd risk meeting one another around tripod barbecue grills and the backs of their bed-lined pickup trucks. That they'd let themselves feel strong. Some of them were arguing, screaming and shoving and still too scared to commit acts of violence. They were arguing over the spray-paint sigils on the sidewalks, the crib-speak ideograms marking which houses would be directly targeted. When Salvage brought the fire. After the grid had been fully dismantled. It had been mapped, carefully, over months, by the hive-mind—determining what should burn first, to Clear the city in just the right way to best effect Salvage-only survival. The unprepared would be left only with indefensible half neighborhoods and ruined plumbing lines. They would starve, or they would leave, and Salvage would take the town.

"It's not clear," Levi said. "Conflicting reports."

But these people didn't know what the sigils meant, and they argued. Some because their houses hadn't been marked, others because theirs had. Most because they'd been too scared to go outside and stop the taggers as they painted their way down the dark street. Earlier. They would have excuses about how, if the taggers had done just *this thing* more, they would have charged across the lawn and beat the hell out of them.

"You worried?" Levi asked. "Being out here?"

"Not now," I said. "Not with this firepower. With the Jacks. We'll get out all right."

Levi looked at the people in the street. "They'll be torn apart, standing around like this when things pick back up."

"Yeah."

One cluster, near the intersection of the substation access road, shouted something at us. They worked up the mob-nerve to approach the Humvee in the street, slowing us down. Began slapping at it, calling for protection. The substation hadn't burned yet, but I could see the bobbing licks of moving flash-lights along its girders and guy lines. Behind the station's stone fence. Salvage was in there, worming.

The other people stepped off their porches. They left their yards and driveways and shambled slowly toward us, toward my now stopped caravan with its gargling motors, its burned-diesel exhaust, and its off-road tires. Their ideas about the National Guard, about what it would do for them, had done for others, on TV in disasters past, drew them to us. We had become the mouth at the bottom of the whirlpool. We were the ones drawing things downstream from all parts of this neighborhood, which was all places to these people.

They were choking off my only way out.

I couldn't take any chances here. The Jacks were behind us, in their smaller rigs, still scared as shit about the dark office and the dead Guards. Their headlights were painting the back of the Humvee with their unease. People were approaching them, too.

"Mary, open the fifty-cal up on the cluster at nine o'clock," I said. "Four, load the ammunition belts."

Levi set down the walkie-talkie and powered up the spotlight. He swung it in a slow arc, backward, lighting up houses and posses in a slow gaze all the way around the Humvee, across the caravan. He stopped on the cluster that had started all of this.

It took the girls a minute to figure out the gun.

"Set," Mary finally said through the porthole, her voice muffled by the sheaves of metal between us.

"Fire at will."

This street was a proto-Place, and its people a proto-Group. A mob.

Several of the Outsiders fell, immediately, when Mary opened up the .50-cal. I couldn't tell if they'd been hit or were diving for cover. She only fired off a few seconds' worth, but as the barrel climbed, propelled upward by its own force, the bullets ate giant holes in the sides of one of these soft houses. She blew the front door apart completely.

We would get better at keeping the barrel level.

The gathering mob, with its pocketknives in sheaths on its belts, with its ideas to get things together and get the neighborhood moving—it went back to a happenstance gathering of the unprepared. It fled back inside.

I couldn't see the lights inside the substation anymore.

We had to sleep. Likely, Salvage had blown at least one more substation. Somewhere. Thanks to fucking Chisolm.

We couldn't leave before the Lull now, but it didn't matter. We had the firepower to make people burn.

I thought about the Wailing Wall. About that message. It couldn't have been real. I couldn't have known then what it was warning me against, which meant the Wall couldn't know. I couldn't have tagged it.

What else hadn't been real? Could we still trust Chance? Its from-the-grave messages?

Why did we take the Humvee? one of my brains asked. *It was an unnecessary expenditure of energy. An unnecessary risk.*

Unless it was real.

Because we had come for answers. And the oracle talked back, to me, through that Wall. We had come to finish off the Last

Man, to finish off Chance. We didn't need anyone anymore, and no one would end up alone.

"No one's going to end up alone," My father had said.

But we did. I did. Levi did.

Everyone ends up alone, standing in nongroups around hospital beds, watching fluids through valves. Watching people cease to be families.

The Jacks were resting in our living room. Smoking cigarettes, reading the *Book* in turns. A pair of them were out back, watching over the Humvee, which looked only like a bamboo grove now, after we'd camouflaged it.

Two of them were sitting apart from the others—Four's girl and the Jack who'd been in the Humvee with us. He had an arm around her, and she was leaning in to his shoulder. They had that slouch. That posture between two kids, when their parents aren't around and they can put their hands where they like.

"Where is the Place," I asked the one who called himself Worm. "Where you were going to regroup?"

He traded a glance with Four's girl. "I don't think . . . sir . . . that we should go there. Even for our gear."

Sir.

"Where is it?" Mary asked.

"It's the high school," he said.

I thought about it. Levi and I had talked about the high school before. Only two ways in and out. Narrow, mischief-deterring windows. But those windows didn't face outward. They were recessed into the exterior walls, and they looked at each other. We guessed you could see some of what went on beyond the campus from those windows, but not much. It would make a bad Place because it would be necessarily nearsighted, except for what you could monitor from the roof. It would be overconfident.

"Why shouldn't we go there?" Levi asked.

The kid looked down. Like he was ashamed. "Because—there're too many Groups there."

"What?"

"There're at least six. Maybe more."

Several Groups in one Place.

"So it's a mess?"

"Yeah."

"We can use that to our advantage."

I dropped a hand on his shoulder. Stood up to go do Something Important. "We'll get the gear, Worm. We'll get it out."

But we had to sleep.

THE BOOK:

"TWO"

SEC. "I," SUBSEC. "C," PROCEDURE "II" ("THE SECOND PHASE")

(cont'd)

[5] (i) Leaving your urban center by wheeled vehicle is likely to be difficult—most highways will be congested beyond use by accident sites, abandoned vehicles, or roadway brigandry. (ii) Use alternate routes. (iii) Avoid interstate highways—use old state-controlled alternatives. (iv) Pre-Event, take the time to learn the whereabouts of nearby paramilitary groups, which may include religious or philosophical sects, racial supremacists, or other paralegal organizations. (v) Avoid routes that will take your Group past these places.

[6] (i) Do not stop to render aid to Outsiders. (ii) Stop to render aid for your own Members only after scout vehicles have ensured the security of the area. (iii) If the security of the area cannot be ensured, deploy your excursion Party on a reconnaissance and assassination mission. (iv) Take no chances. (v) If your Group must appeal to other travelers for aid, minimize the number of Members exposed when doing so, as it is likely that the Member flagging for help will come under weapons or debris fire. (vi) Conceal your Group as much as possible. (vii) Other motorists are more likely to help a single person or a small Group than a large one. (viii) Be prepared to ambush those who stop to render aid.

[7] (i) Expect roadblocks. (ii) If a roadblock catches your pilot crew by surprise, then there is a possibility that your vehicle will, in turn, catch at least some of the roadblock crew by surprise. Use your vehicle as a weapon in this

instance. (iii) As soon as possible, open fire or deploy your Party to neutralize the roadblock crew. (iv) You will likely sustain casualties, and the vehicle will almost certainly be rendered inoperable. In a desperate situation, the sacrifice of the first vehicle may ensure the passage of the second.

[8] (i) Do not stop for rest. (ii) Alternate your crews if necessary. (iii) Proceed directly to your Place. (iv) Stopping at residences to Forage will likely result in death, for each will be its own siege warfare situation. (v) Only unattended fields of produce or grain are worthy of Forage. (vi) Under these circumstances, keep the vehicles constantly ready. (vii) Do not turn off their engines, even to refuel.

[9] (i) Expect resistance in every location. (ii) When you reach your Place, expect resistance.

CHAPTER ELEVEN

have you decided?" Four asked. Levi and I had decided to let her do this. To make her do this. We needed to commit her fully.

Four's girl spoke for the Jacks. "Yes."

We were in a line: Levi, Mary, Four, and I. The Jacks were in another line, standing across from us in the living room. Fluff and Edmund were weaving and rubbing the Jacks' legs. They didn't care about this.

It was a game of Red Rover, only we were letting the Jacks call themselves out, instead of doing it for them. We were making them betray their old selves to the line of linked arms across the field, where they'd be knocked off their asses and kicked out of the game.

"Circe," Four's girl said. Who knew how many names she'd taken before this, if she'd taken nicknames. If she'd tried out several new names once she joined her first Group, settling at last on whatever she'd called herself. We didn't care—didn't want to know.

Levi wrote the new name down on a stenographer's pad.

It wasn't for anything—we wouldn't even keep it. But we wanted them to see us taking note. Making things official.

"Next," Four prompted.

"Matthew."

Mary looked at him. It didn't sound new.

"From the Bible," he said. "The Gospels."

"We know," I said.

I looked at Levi. In the Bible, Matthew had also been called Levi.

He nodded.

Next.

"Mark."

Another Gospel. They were probably close. Had been Before. Like Adam and me.

We'd have to watch that.

Next.

"Penelope"

then

"Silo"

and Worm said

"Merlin"

but then another said

"God."

We stopped.

"God?" I asked.

"Yes," he said.

"No."

"What—"

"No."

"But, it's mine. I chose. You said I get to choose."

"Choose something else."

"Why?"

We all looked at him.

"Because it's stupid," I told him. "We're not playing some game here. I don't know what you think you can do with 'God,' but it won't work out the way you think. The way we need it to."

"It's full of the wrong ideas," Levi offered, playing Good Cop, "about what it means to be a new you. A better you."

"It will fail you, which is us," Four said.

I looked at her.

"Fine," God said. "I'll be Zero."

"Next."

"Pump."

Next.

"Voice."

Last.

"Luke."

So there were three of them. Matthew, Mark, and Luke. We'd have to be sure. Make them realize, like God, that we weren't playing games.

There was an occult logic to High School Parking. Not in the lots themselves, but among the drivers. There was a tradition, among students, regarding the esoteric orders and hierarchies of filling the lots. The meaning of self in a suburban high school, where the kids drove cars their parents bought, trading fender benders during their lunch-hour release the same way they had once traded baseball cards.

Visibility was important to cracking the codes—the ciphers—of behavior and movement in a parking lot. Could your peers see your assertion of self, your car, as they paced their ways toward the two sets of student-containing doors? There was never, in any school, a direct path between the doors.

Or were you too far back, in the hinterland? In some back-lot wasteland that delayed arrival and departure and the escape for lunch. It was a competition for control of resources—namely, the narrow lanes in and out of the lot. How quickly could you enact your Exit Strategy, to get yourself and your friends out? How well could you be seen doing this? Could you be the one with the fast car, who can do the thing, who can get people out, out, out?

We decided to obey the barricades. Someone in the Jacks' old high school had taken the sawhorsed, orange-painted traffic barricades, stenciled to read SECURITY with black aerosol paint, from the storerooms where they were kept between football games, school plays, and dances. Before Everything, the barricades emerged to usher traffic in new directions, after normal school hours, when the daylight rules of parking no longer applied. When we were no longer allowed to go to the same places, in the same ways, as we were when the *body politic* was ruled only by students. We preferred it our way—having parents around, after normal hours, changed everything. Because we had it all figured out.

The arrangement of the barricades, approaching the lanes into and out of the parking lots, looked chaotic. I couldn't tell if that was intentional, or if it evidenced different Groups enacting different strategies of perimeter defense. The point was that it would deliver Outsiders into the parking lot in the fashion those inside had deemed best.

Playing along, following the barricades, was part of the Plan. We hadn't brought the Humvee. Levi was back at the House of Cards, monitoring 'casts. Those that were left, anyway. He had Penelope on the walkie-talkie. Silo and Zero were monitoring his perimeter. We wanted to look like we were petitioning for

Addition, or offering to establish New Trade. We didn't want these Groups' nascent Administrations to be stressed by our presence.

For Jon and me, at our high school, parking science had been more than the struggle for the right spot. It had been about power, and social authority, and what was given you from On High—what you couldn't change. Like Calvinism, perhaps. Like predestination, and learning to live happily while being poor and foredamned, which we studied in World History II.

Because we were sophomores, we had a lower place on the Great Chain of Being. We couldn't park in the main lot, which was reserved for juniors and seniors. There were already too many of them, because things were on the upswing then—lots of jobs, so lots of new families in the suburbs, buying cars for their children. Getting them "situated."

We'd brought the Jacks' trucks. I was in one cab, driving in the point position, Circe riding shotgun beside me. Matthew, Mark, and Luke were in the now emptied bed behind us, obscured from view by the camper shell. It had been Circe's truck. Judging by the decals on the back window, she had spent a lot of her time in the Future Farmers of America. Probably breeding mini lop rabbits and hauling feed for class projects to the school district's ranch outside of town. My sister had been in the FFA, and she had done things like tattoo the rabbits' ears with a dyed-and-needled hole punch. She had marked them with a single letter, like a pointillist graffito-stencil—her first initial. The mark of She Who Was All Things to her rabbits. She had done things like mix fertilizers under faculty supervision. She had participated in farm-risk-assessment assignments, like how much grain in one silo will cause spontaneous grain-dust combustion. Volunteer firefighters had helped her and the other students put out the fires in their miniature silos, and I had stood with my mother, with the other families, and watched the little buildings burn.

It made sense. Circe had to have learned how to cook somewhere, and in the FFA she'd have access to things like sodium nitrate and potassium chloride. My sister had spent a semester in a work-study program about dairy farm maintenance. She'd learned to use nitric acid to clean the scabbed deposits from the vacuum lines that milked the cows.

Circe would have needed nitric acid, too. The recipe called for it. Some adolescents join gangs, some smoke. Some cook dynamite.

There had been a lottery to get a parking sticker in the overflow lot, which was behind the football fields. I had not won the right to the lot, but Jon had, so we pooled our resources. His access and my car. Our lives became about arrival time. We awoke before sunrise, made time to stop for donuts at the shop around the corner from our housing development. It had gone up in a little strip mall long after we'd stopped using our fort. After we'd given up on the grocery store that had displaced us. There were even fewer tall grasses in that field then.

Despite Merlin's concerns, it wasn't so odd that there was more than one Group in the school—even if it was a mistake. There always had been. Sophomores, juniors, seniors—each having Placed the school themselves. Each class enacting different politics, oblivious to the others because the student body was too large. You couldn't struggle for power beyond your caste—it would spread your resources too thin. It was illogical, for the rules of the Great Chain of Being were inviolate. One might as well have been scheming against God, to get rid of the idea of The Elect, and predestination, and being fucked from the get-go as a commoner without the right name.

Jon and I made sure to get to school early—an hour, at least—so we could secure one of the closest parking spots to the long, gravel trail that led from the overflow lot to the back entrance. We would sleep in the car, in turns. Keeping watch. Waiting to be first inside, once the vice principal unlocked the doors.

But we had others with us. Mary drove the other truck, Four riding shotgun beside her. Voice, Pump, and Merlin awaited orders in the bed, under the other camper shell.

Mary's truck had been Penelope's. I didn't know why she drove a truck, why she picked a truck, newer than Circe's, when her father had said "Choose." Penelope did not have the look of the FFA—I didn't know what history to imagine for her. But it didn't matter—she had offered the keys readily when Mary asked for them.

"Park there," Circe directed. This was her lot, and she knew its secrets.

THE BOOK:

"THREE" ("ARRIVAL")

[1] (i) When you reach your Place, consider it enemy territory. Nearby Groups may very likely have already begun surveillance operations, scouting others' likely Places and lying in wait to Forage their lives and materials when Group vigilance will naturally be at its lowest since the Event. (ii) Arriving successfully at your Place is, indeed, a time for celebration, but you have not Arrived until you have secured the area. (iii) Leadership will not be reassigned or decentralized until the Place is secure.

[2] (i) In the event that your Place belonged to an Outsider under the premises of Old Trade, you will need to remove him or her. (ii) If your Place contains arable land, it will be to your benefit to first approach the once-owner and attempt to Add him or her to your Group, as his or her expertise with the land will be to your benefit. (iii) In the unfortunate event that the once-owner objects, you will need to eliminate him or her and his or her family, for requisitioning land from those that still believe they own it will only lead to rebellion, revenge, or warfare. (iv) Though you may feel vestigial guilt for "stealing" this land, remember that Old Trade "ownership" was underwritten by now unstable law enforcement and military personnel. (v) Under the premises of New Trade, "ownership" is the ability to deter Outsiders from acquiring what you do not wish them to acquire.

[3] (i) When you have secured your Place, your primary Group concerns are food, water, shelter, and reconnaissance. (ii) As soon as possible, designate a new task-based engineering Leader. (iii) He or she must begin immediately securing the

necessary apparatus for resource security, such as wells,
shadoofs, irrigation channels, Foraging Parties, etc.

[4] (i) The engineering Leader's other primary task is the
construction of temporary shelter—tents, natural shelters,
or other forms of simple housing will suffice at this point.
(ii) Your inclination will be simply to rest once you Arrive.
(iii) Disregard your inclination.

[5] (i) Muster a number of your combatant Members for defense and
reconnaissance. Theirs will be the task of ensuring the
safety of the engineering operations as well as scouting for
nearby Groups. (ii) Unless presented with a life-or-death
defense situation, your reconnaissance Party should not
engage other Groups or Parties.

CHAPTER TWELVE

Walking toward the school doors, Luke treated Circe like she was pregnant. She had taken her hair out of its braid, on Mary's orders, before we left the HOC. Unbound, it was long and straight and chestnut-colored, the same color as her boots. It was less *severe*, Mary had explained to me. This was not operations hair—this was girlfriend hair, and it would help to disarm the Outsiders in the school. Circe *looked* like she needed to be worried about. Like she was a liability and we knew it, but we weren't *hard* enough to have devoted ourselves so fully to our Plan that we would have left her behind like we should have because she was an unnecessary expenditure of energy.

Luke walked on her pregnant side, her right side, where she carried two emptied cans of condensed milk in a sling. The cans had been soldered together and filled with iron filings and other bits of shrapnel. They had also been packed with dynamite.

Luke hovered his hand over the grenade's homespun womb, and Matthew watched Mark, watching Luke. And the thing was, Circe let them watch, because the important question, if the

Jacks had all been Secondary—Auxiliary Demolitions—was where their Primaries were. Where was "Ishmael" while Luke stayed with her in the darkness?

Levi and I had talked about families and couples. We approved, because they were insurance. They kept people motivated.

And children even more so, if we could figure out how to deliver them.

Which is why, when we first got back to the HOC after Foraging the Humvee, after Levi and I had a chance to see what was among the Jacks' meager equipment, in the backs of their trucks, I ordered Circe to bring a grenade. I intended to see it delivered.

She would be the mother of many more.

"What the fuck you want?" the sentry asked.

He wasn't being combative. He spoke with a Latino accent, and he had tied a traditional paisley-and-filigree bandanna across his face. A black one. A junior in the high school, my guess. Before.

I didn't flinch when his partner raised a .40-cal lackadaisically. I didn't let anyone else flinch, either. This one was wearing the same type of bandanna. His hair was dyed blond, and it was spiked.

I sized them up for a minute. Made a show of it. "You two Salvage?"

"What's it matter?" the second sentry asked, milder of voice.

Good Cop, Bad Cop.

I looked, with Four and Mary, at the football field. We could see it now, this close to the school, beyond the walnut trees that had blocked it from view in the parking lot. There were two or three clusters of people working the field, lit by car-battery-powered utility lights. They were tilling it by hand, five-gallon buckets—of herbicide, no doubt—waiting on the sidelines. They hadn't gotten very far.

I looked back at the sentries.

"It doesn't matter," I said. "Just looking to set some things up."

"What kinds of things?" the first sentry asked.

"Are you petitioning Addition?" the second one added.

Mary lit a cigarette, made a show of looking around. Let them *see* her.

"Just Trade," I said. "Intel. We come from the university. From the firefight. Picked a few things up from the Rats and from the Wall on our way out."

They watched Mary.

"Haven't heard any of it coming through what's fucking left of Salvage, so thought we'd try to set some things up, with who-ever's staying. Spread the Good Word."

"You're Group?" the first sentry asked.

"Party. Some of us. Found these others running from the Guard."

They looked at the Jacks. At Circe.

"Hey, fuck," First said. "You're 'Sons of Man.'"

Matthew and Mark stopped watching Luke. They watched the gun in the hands of the second sentry, waiting, waiting.

I watched them. They'd named themselves, their Group. Not their Place. They'd thought ahead—they would be nomads, Bedouins. A Place in constant movement, expecting, I'd guess, from before the get-go that if they'd simply tried to name their Place, the school, it wouldn't take. The borders would be re-drawn too often, sharing the Place with Outside Groups. Who knew what underground culture had grown from Salvage, in the school, among the frustrated students. They would have planned, cooperatively, the contestation, the multiple Placing of the school, post-Event.

Whatever was going on inside, it's what the high school hive-mind had always intended. Phantom Cell Structure. Noise.

A bad idea.

"Why the fuck you got A's on your faces?" Second asked.

"Guard put them there," Merlin said. " 'Asylum,' the shitheads said."

"You went *to* the Guard?" Second asked.

"Your A's are wildstyle," First said. "Fucking Guard write wildstyle?"

"Weren't you supposed to blow them up?" Second asked.

"We didn't have any fucking choice," Matthew said. He was the odd one out—the ugliest of the three. He had a habit of watching Mark watch Luke. "We're not Ishmael's Primaries. They never came. We were left to the fucking wind."

Ishmael's Primaries. A Final Leader. A new self born, perhaps, from AP English classes, reading *Moby-Dick,* and attending Sunday school.

Circe had been watching First quietly. "You're Prometheus, right?" she asked him, tucking her chestnut hair behind her ears.

I looked at him, wondering what he'd done, what Boy Scout troop he'd been in, what tasks he'd carried out under adolescent orders, to earn the name? Who, like me, had given it to him?

"Promo, now," he said.

Circe could have known him from English class. They might have read *A Separate Peace,* and *Julius Caesar,* and Aeschylus at the same time. He might have looked at her, over the corners of his books, during those times when he didn't care that she was FFA. That she was rich, and white.

I looked at her, the way he might have, and I remembered

flowers—from *Mythology*. Promo, with that heat in his eyes, remembered the fire, smoldering those years between seventh grade, when the school system made students read it, and now.

"Does CLO.WN still hold?" she asked. "You still CLO.WN?"

"Wait," I said. Mary and Four took a step back with me, from the Jacks. This was rehearsed. "You're CLO.WN?"

The second one raised his gun again.

"What the fuck?"

"No," I said. "This is your Place. We'll bug out."

"No, what the hell?"

"Hold up."

"No, it's cool. Good luck."

The second sentry thrust his gun forward. Pulled it back. "What *the fuck*? You're not just afraid of CLO.WN."

I traded looks with Four. Mary was making a show of watching the perimeter. She looked at the workers in the field, unprotected.

I looked around, too. Watching for eavesdroppers. "All right, look. You've been called out. CLO.WN's been called out. It's on the Wall. Showed up sometime after Chisolm's sign-off. After the hive had already been set to start Clearing the town."

"What?" Promo said.

"No fucking way."

"No one knows us."

I raised my hands. Took another step away from the gun. Some of the Jacks sidestepped slowly. Those that weren't Sons of Man. Backing away on their own.

I shrugged. "Somebody must know your Place. Somebody who wants to Clear you out. Remove some competition, I'm guessing. You'll go when the mobs go, unless you've got a hell of a lot of Primaries in there."

I gestured toward the field. "Your Secondaries are going to get eaten alive out here."

They didn't know what to do.

"So, take that for free," I said, waving Four and Mary farther back. "We don't want in on the mess. Won't join the hive."

"No, wait," the second sentry said. He lowered his gun. "What else you got?"

I shook my head. "I got plenty, but what in hell you got to justify the risk of coming in and getting Cleared along with you?"

"We got some lab gear." He looked at Circe. "It was stashed here when their operation began."

I let my fingers touch the hilt of the sword. Let the wan light wink on the blade's dark blood.

"All right."

I stepped forward.

"Make it fucking quick. You bastards are on a timer now."

They admitted us without a search. Which was the Plan.

"Hey," the first one said to Circe as she preceded Luke inside. "Ishmael came back. I guess after bugging out on you. He's still got a Place, on the second floor."

Circe said "Good."

I was fifteen when I left. It was in the summer after my sopho-more year, which meant I'd already studied the Celestial Spheres, but I hadn't yet met Her. I hadn't yet received my car. The knight-hood was at its height. I left Jon and Adam, which screwed the summer's D&D campaigns, since they'd be a man down, and I went overseas. Exchange program. Spending my parents' money and trying to live with honor in foreign countries.

This was before we ceased to be a family.

In Italy, outside Rome, we toured the catacombs. We went underground, into the dark of the earth, but unlike Orpheus, we could look back. The wrong corridors had been roped off to keep us on course, to keep us in line on our way to the bottom, to have a chat with Odysseus and eat a few pomegranate seeds. I spent a lot of my time ignoring the displayed skulls and tucked femurs to look askance at the girls in our group. Some I knew, from other schools near Dallas. The others came from Indianapolis, so I worried less about the repercussions with these. I already knew, after I looked back at them in the darkness, that I would lose them. I was foredamned, fucked from the get-go, so it didn't matter what I did during my three days in the underworld.

I tried to keep that in mind.

Promo led us through a hallway, through his Group's wing. The other sentry, the blond one, had gone to corral the Secondaries.

By flashlight, black-masked workers used crowbars to open the lockers along the wall. They'd already torn open the majority, leaving books, mirrors, boxes of tampons, and cans of body spray in categorized piles, like snowdrifts. A few of the unopened lockers, dented and bent along their hinges and near the lock, had been greasepainted with sigils. One of the workers was pasting sheets from some *Book* on these lockers with a paintbrush and a bowl of egg whites—

You weren't supposed to do anything to the vaults, you weren't even supposed to take pictures of the corpses behind the Plexiglas, but we did it anyway, our fingers over our cameras' flashes, creating momentary pulses of red light as the bulbs shone through our flesh.

—We marched all the way through, following the barricades, going where we were supposed to in the dark, following our guide, following Promo. I kept one eye on him and the other on the Jacks, watching for the sign. I needed to know when Promo was going to become a problem. When he was going to lead us in a direction to *actually* trade intel with his Final Leader.

He waved us into a classroom—

Part of the exchange program was to spend time in other schools. A small college in Budapest, a satellite school in Vienna. Some art co-op in Florence. Or something. The point being, to demonstrate how much harder it was to go to school somewhere else, however hard we thought it was at home. No one had told us about relative measure, cultural normativity, and the problem with seeing something foreign at all, since it is necessarily domestic once it hits your brain.

—So, I wasn't surprised. Neither did Mary seem to be, but Four stayed outside, with Circe. She couldn't go in.

"Hey," Promo called to one of the others in the classroom. This one was neither masked nor painted, and he had to stop stitching the wound in his patient's arm to look up.

"Where the hell's Bob?" Promo asked.

The surgeon shrugged. "Recon."

His patient was laid atop three desks shoved together to make a bed. He wasn't moving. Others were waiting against the wall, their faces obscured by yellow or white bandannas. None of these wore black. They waited quietly, patiently, without moving, their heads slumped against their chests. A few were leaning against each other, which I remembered—boys and girls using their shoulders to flirt, when they were free to lounge where they liked during the lunch hour. It was a way they could date, without the hassle, because they were just "friends." The contact made them so, and a few would later fuck, when they found themselves in the same community college, having elected not to go off to some university, but to stay. Because there was a good reason. There was always a good reason—

They had tools, the men in the factory at the top of that hill, somewhere in northern Italy. Where they used industrial lathes to carve alabaster vases, which ended up as pencil holders or jewelry boxes for our parents, when we got back to Texas, or Indiana, or wherever. After my father died, I took back the one I had bought for him. I Salvaged it. The workers had alabaster dust and buckets of lubricant and cigarettes around flammable things, but it didn't matter. The only thing they might burn was the whole damn hill.

—These CLO.WN surgeons had dentist's tools, which they would have gotten, no doubt, from some grocery store—where you could get those things. They'd taken them from—

the bastards who'd taken the land outside the fort. Who'd acquired the tall grasses and invaded for resources.

—The surgeons had ceramics tools and Dremel tools wired into car batteries.

A different surgeon was mapping a different patient with a greasepaint marker. He was making sigils, and identifying lines, and outlining important parts. He was marking the areas where he'd missed, with the syringe lying on the desk beside him, when he'd practiced stabbing his victim in the heart, so he'd be ready in case one of his Group's Primaries suffered heart failure. The school nurse kept one of these syringes under lock, just in case.

I wasn't surprised that he'd removed all of her clothes. He couldn't very well have begun exploring, with those *lathes and tools,* her curves and whitenesses and *alabaster* skin, without doing so. He couldn't otherwise determine the appropriate *pitch and camber to make vases and penholders and miscellaneous receptacles.* He couldn't know what to do next time, when she would be alive and when it would be a matter of romance, and not teaching himself battlefield surgery—

One of the girls, from our school, had come to use her shoulders in the room that I shared with one of the other guys. She had come in her

pajamas, to make contact, because it was after hours, and she could do
what she wanted here.

—Here, there was a new politics, because there were no parents
around to fuck the Great Chain of Being. To mess with the order
of things. I didn't know enough to be anything other than casual,
to pretend this was normal, so I only glanced at the security
guard's corpse in the corner. They would have taken his radio after
they began Arriving at the school, after the Event. They'd had to
consider their Place enemy territory, and he was only the first of
many on which they'd have to learn to play doctor.

Because what else could they have done? The nurse's office
was in someone else's territory. It wasn't part of their Place.

Later, we crossed the border from the catacombs into Austria,
where we necessarily said good-bye. We had only been a Group
for a short time, some weeks, in Italy, where we'd established our
own body politic, where we'd been parented by only two trip co-
ordinators. In Italy, we'd been allowed to do what we wanted with
our currency. We'd been allowed to wander the Grand Canal in
Venice, where, in one instance, the girl who had worn pajamas
into my room had been chased by Outsiders. Two of our Primaries managed to chase them off, but not before she fled straight
into the brackish water of a back-alley canal. We'd been allowed
to sneak onto hotel rooftops, to smoke cigarettes at night and sit
in closer proximity than we would during the daylight. I'd found
my way into a bar, at one point, to order a glass of wine. Which is
what my old fantasy-book heroes and Romantic idols would
have done. While they smoked their pipes, which I'd already
learned how to do.

• • •

We couldn't have a guide around us for this operation, so we killed Promo.

I'd gotten the signal from Mark. Promo was going to take us in the wrong direction, when we reached the end of the hall, so we needed to solidify ourselves, to free us up from being found out, or forced to actually Trade intel—

We were on our way to a small town outside Vienna, where I stayed with a family in a hillside château. One of the surrounding mountains was missing an entire, symmetrical wedge of trees. We were told the devil had taken them.

—I could have done it. I could have ordered Mary to do it. I could have ordered her to order one of the Jacks to do it, but she needed to order it herself. All of this needed to happen.

Matthew borrowed a knife and a last-ditch syringe from Pump—

From the man who owned the château, for a hike through the trees, around the property.

—Matthew used the knife to cut *the sticky greenbrier when it grabbed at his sleeves,* and he watched in the dark, *on the way back, as the man pointed to the slab where he and his son were going to build a family chapel. Before the son died. Before I came home to a dying father.*

—Before he could rethink things, Matthew pulled his shirttail over his face and then cut Promo across the arm, so he would turn his head. He jammed the syringe into Promo's neck and depressed the plunger.

We left Promo around the corner. We wanted it to look like a border skirmish, and here, he wasn't far from the morgue ward, where he could be used to teach his surgeons better ways of bringing broken things back together.

Circe watched Luke watching Mark watching Matthew. Seeing things in reverse. Mary cupped Matthew's face in her alabaster palm. She took the knife, cleaned it on Promo's shirt, and gave it back to him. She took Promo's pistol and shoved it behind her waistband, the barrel in line with the crack of her ass. I wondered about Matthew's hobbies, about his two friends, about the new girl and reducing oneself, one's friendships, by sex. I wondered if he knew yet what a woman's fingers on his face might mean.

"What you did was right."

We ducked into a dark classroom when some skirmish broke out. In some distant part of the school. It was difficult to gauge the number of participants because the gunfire echoed, and no doubt, many combatants weren't using firearms. They may have been fighting to find out who took the fire from Prometheus.

I knew what Luke was thinking, looking at Circe. Looking at the grenade asleep in its sling—

When I had met Her. After Jon had met his Her. When things changed among all three of us—Adam and Jon and me—my worries shifted. Sex was everything, and that meant, every time, that She and I were making grenades of our own, between us. Even if we used things like condoms and gels, because we were terrified of what we might make together. We'd had scares of our own, because we were too stupid to recognize the difficulty in creating children. We knew only our fear.

—so I knew what Luke was thinking, staring at that sling, at Circe's unbound hair. He knew the first Circe to use the name had given birth to a minotaur. He wondered how he could love such a thing as she could make. As he made with her.

• • •

When we finally arrived, in what had originally been the corridor of the Sons of Man, we ran. Mark took the point position on my orders, to direct our course, and we ran across enemy territory that had new lines, new cardinal measures, that the Jacks didn't even understand anymore. They'd been away too long, and territory shifted too readily in the high school. There was an explosion downstairs. In the half-light of a passing window, we saw the buckets of fertilizer burning on the football field.

Another Party found us, running in their own direction, away from their own things. Their faces were obscured by black-on-white paisley-and-filigree bandannas. They lifted the same guns we did, there in the corridor.

"Wait—" Circe said. "—Ishmael."

They lowered their guns. We didn't.

He stepped out from behind his ghost-faced escort.

"It's us," she said. "What the fuck?"

"Who the hell are these others?" Ishmael asked.

"Additions," Luke said, a butane lighter between his fingers. He stood just behind Circe's sling.

"Where the *fuck* were you guys?" Matthew asked.

Ishmael sent a runner back the way they'd come. He slipped his bandanna off his face. He was pretty, with black hair and blue, blue eyes. They drew in the weak window-light. He looked surprised to have caught his Secondaries, floating downstream.

"We were . . . caught." He shook his head. "It doesn't matter. You were supposed to wait."

The way Circe was looking at him—this wasn't just "Ishmael."

He looked at us. "Lower your guns, assholes."

I didn't send any signals. I let Mary lower her guns on her own. I couldn't look like a Leader here.

"You didn't *fucking* come," Circe said.

"I came back," Ishmael said.

He was their Leader. He would have been the one to convince them to start cooking. Got them into Salvage. First Circe, then Luke—who would have brought Matthew and Mark, even though they *weren't invited to Adam's house to play D&D*.

"You . . . fuck you, Jason," Circe said.

Ishmael reeled.

He said "Morgan."

"We were nearly blown apart by the Guard," Luke said. "By our own fucking trap."

And Luke had stayed with Circe in the darkness.

"Shut up, Carson," Jason said to Luke.

Wait.

Ishmael was probably the one with the fast car, the one who could get her out, out, out of this shit town with its shit farms and shit people and shit family businesses. Its shit college students and their shit venues because there was nothing to do underage but hang out on the Strip and sell pot.

Circe's hands were shaking. "I can't believe—"

I imagined that Luke had listened to her—in algebra class, maybe—when she might have complained about how easily jealous Ishmael could become, for what idiotic reasons. Luke might have listened, commiserated, because he would have been competing for resources, namely the ways in-and-out of Circe.

I didn't want to hear these names.

"You know what, Jason," Luke said, stepping out from behind Circe. "You know *fucking what?*"

But Circe wasn't an overflow lot. There wasn't some back road upon which Luke could arrive early to effect his exit strategy. There's only one way underground, and that's the direct path, in front of the school. Its entrances stoplighted by things like boyfriends and the order of authority in the Group.

Ishmael grabbed Luke and shoved him against the wall.

And when Ishmael had convinced Circe to cook dynamite, she convinced Luke, who followed her underground because what other fucking option did he have?

They're not wearing paint.

Luke shoved back. With his knife.

No.

"Hiram!"

There was thunder coming up the stairs behind us.

Luke took a bullet to the face, from Ishmael's posse. Pump took one to the chest. I hadn't had time to create histories for all of them yet. I hadn't had time to care that they would die, which would have to be good enough.

Four grabbed Circe and pulled her against the wall. Mary and I *murdered* the other Sons of Man—the rest of Ishmael's posse. We didn't *eliminate* them because we were using the wrong words. The wrong names. We were our wrong selves here. This was wrong.

Merlin and Voice ducked into the chemistry classroom. I saw Voice throw a chair through the window. Matthew climbed onto the fire escape, waiting to be the first one down. With the gear, from six Groups, from a lot of clandestine fucking Salvage, when it was handed to him. Mark was watching Matthew not watching Luke.

I sent Mary through, to see to the gear, with an armful of the Sons of Man's guns. I waited with Four in the hallway, waiting for the storm climbing the stairs. She planted a slow kiss on Morgan's forehead, who stared at her with wide, unseeing eyes.

They lit the grenade and threw it down the hallway. When it exploded, it tore the doors from the lockers and collapsed the ceiling. Born without a father. Born out of wedlock. There was no option but to destroy it. I knew this.

We heard the storm screaming as the shrapnel flew into it, defying the laws of normal motion.

We weren't wearing paint. They were using their old names.

What we did was wrong.

THE BOOK:

"THREE" ("ARRIVAL")

(cont'd)

[6] (i) Should the Party encounter potential Additions, these
Additions must present a worthwhile contribution to the
Place, such as necessary knowledge, valuable equipment, or
the capability of physical labor. (ii) Accepting Secondary
Membership Additions will be determined by the number of
such Members already in your Group. (iii) The precise ratio
of Secondary to Primary members will vary from Group to
Group, based on such factors as the martial stability of
surrounding territory, the abundance or availability of
resources, or the need for manual-labor workforces. (iv) The
Leader should not authorize a Forage for others' supplies,
should the Party encounter individuals with such in their
possession. (v) The reasoning behind this is that now that
you have Arrived at your Place, it is important not to
establish military authority on the idea of wanton
barbarity, for this can lead to divisions of power between
combatant-Members and noncombatants. (vi) You must maintain
your combatants as a militia, not an army, for they must be
as invested in the equality of the Group and the Place as
are working noncombatants.

I.

[1] (i) You will require Special Days and Monuments. Both
strengthen your Narrative.

I.A.

"SPECIAL DAYS"

[1] (i) Your first Special Day should be "Arrival Day"—an after-the-fact remembrance of your Arrival—and it should be a Day of Rest. This is a Day for telling and retelling Narratives of the Evacuation and Arrival. This is a Day of celebration. (ii) Watch rotation is not a violation of the terms of rest.

[2] (i) If you have fermented drink, tobacco, or esoteric herbs and chemicals among your supplies, offer these for use upon Arrival Day. (ii) Secondary Members with musical skill, storycraft, or other Expressions-of-Society abilities should contribute these to Society on Arrival Day (and other Days to follow), thus graduating into Primary Membership. (iii) From this point forward, it will be part of their contributions to arrange new material that is a specific expression of Place-culture instead of recycling Old Trade expressions.

[3] (i) Do not restrict the content of Place-expression, even when it seems to threaten prosperity. It is necessary that Members express their frustrations and losses. Doing so, in fact, strengthens prosperity, contrary to what you may think. (ii) Censorship initiates Collapse and Failure, at any stage in a Place's history.

CHAPTER THIRTEEN

Iistening to the walkie-talkie, I heard phantasmal half conversations between Groups, on the way back to the HOC. We had the Jacks' gear. We were situated.

There was more static than normal, and it sang between transmissions. Everyone sounded distant. A few of the clearer voices were running amplifiers, which made them sound electric. It gave them more range, the first word on the waves across the ocean—the first draw that would suck at distant ships, the Charybdis in charge of everyone's directions, even if no one knew. Even if everyone thought he had dead-reckoned his own course. Even if it would take a thousand miles to get sucked between a rock and a hard place.

I thought about tin-can voices, playing telephone in grade school with a line of twine. Mostly what you heard was your own voice, sounding hollow. Foreign. You were someone else when you spoke into the can, and it was nice to hear your own voice, like staring at that mirror, sounding distance in the dark, making noise. Wondering if Bloody Mary would ever show up.

• • •

When I was young, when we were still a family, I heard those amped CB voices out in the dark. Out west, where there were no lights on the highways, and you could see every star while your sisters slept on the bench, in the van, beside you. A road trip. Family vacation. Your mother's head nodding, knowingly, as she dozed with the highway next to your father.

Back then, I read only fantasy novels and books about space. NASA technical manuals describing the space shuttle, its SRBs, pitch and yaw, and reentry. I planned on joining the air force, to pilot shuttles. Out there in space, where there was no one.

But in the dark, in the van, I didn't read. I looked at those too-many stars, winking darkly through the tinted glass, and I breathed deeply when clouds of dark smoke from my father's pipe moved over me. It was dusty, out west, and you could see devils twirling when truckers' lights painted them, out there among the brush. My father drove, the spill of the headlights the only measure against unseen holes in the earth. We listened to old recordings of Hank Williams, and Willie Nelson, and Randy Travis, because that was what he liked. Songs for Orpheus on his way down, into the Texas darkness, through the tobacco smoke, and over the holes in the earth. He explained to me then why some of the voices on his CB—which he kept on, even when we didn't need it—sounded so strange. He told me about the amps, about how they broke FCC regulations. Between songs, I would listen to those voices, to that language I didn't know yet.

I was little then. I didn't know better.

Levi's voice cut through the halftones and static. "Copy, Party, this is HOC. Go ahead."

"Target acquired," I said. "Over."

"Copy, Party. Did you sustain casualties?"

Yes.

"Affirmative."

He was quiet for a minute. I listened to the ghosts on the waves talking about Dallas. They were explaining, in their one-sided conversations, that it was to blame for the glow to the southeast. They were still driving their trucker rigs. Still shipping bullshit nowhere, across state lines, to sell to no one.

"Copy. The rest of the stations have gone. The Northern Lights are over."

"Copy," I said, watching the truck's headlights paint glowing road onto the band of darkness in front of us.

"What's your ETA?"

On Scripture Street, I saw one uniformed cop, his massive, flashlight-cum-club waving—a torch in the darkness. There were others with him, marching, in civilian clothes. They moved up a sidewalk, toward someone's front porch. There were other flash-lights glowing, on other porches, all the way down the block.

"Ten minutes."

"Copy, Party. You are not cleared for deviation. I don't want any spontaneous recon. Do you copy?"

"Copy, HOC."

"Salvage has started Clearing. We're going to have to wait."

"Copy. See you in ten."

"Copy."

"Levi?"

"Yeah?"

"I'm all right."

The static washed, like waves ashore, between us. One wave carried all the way from across the sea. From the Charybdis we couldn't see coming, sailing so far away.

• • •

We left Zero and Silo on watch once we got back. It was getting late, and we'd need to start a rotation soon. But not yet. Matthew and Mark stowed the new gear while Merlin and Voice took inventory. Everyone needed something to do. I made each responsible for something. *Only Patrol Leaders could carry compasses. I needed them all to be important to the troop.*

Inside, there were candles. The black-and-white offered only static light. The digital, of course, had no power. I handed Circe off to Penelope, and she went willingly. She had nothing-distances to stare, to orient herself in the darkness, to think about who'd died, and how. Penelope was sounding things back to her, even if Circe wasn't sounding them herself.

Levi, Mary, Four, and I gathered in the kitchen. An ashtray between us on the table. We all smoked.

"When are we getting out of here?" Four asked.

"The Lull's no good anymore," Levi said. "Penelope watched a cluster of backpacked undergrads heading down Broadway, toward Thirty-five."

"What does that mean?" Mary asked. We could hear Penelope speaking softly in the other room. I could hear her humming.

Levi looked at Mary. "First of all, what you all did was right."

He had no idea, not yet.

I looked down at the table, but that was a mistake, too. I looked back up, to take a drag of that awful cigarette. Four was staring at me, her expression soft as she read the lines of my face.

"But to answer your question, it was an exodus. Dorm kids, I'd guess. They didn't make it far, open like that during the Lull."

"How far?" Mary asked.

"The cemetery."

"So we'll wait out the second wave," I said. "We've got a lot more firepower than we'd planned on."

"We could use it now. To get out," Mary said.

"Yes," Four said.

"Waste of ammunition," I said. "The trucks would take unnecessary damage. The Jacks' chemicals could make a fifty-foot crater in all directions if they took fire."

"What about Circe?" Mary asked. "The *Book* doesn't have any Narrative for her. For this."

"I know," I said.

I looked at them. At Mary, their White Mary who could lay her hands on anything. Make anything make sense. And Four, with those serpents, with her darkness, the small voice in the bookstore office, who had calmed Circe, when she had been only Morgan, waiting for her boyfriend while the Guard shelled the living fuck out of the bookstore and the Auditorium Building. Who had calmed her again, arms around Circe's shoulders, by yanking her out of the high school hallway. Who had been there with hands after Luke had gone. Becoming Carson again, in those last important moments.

If we weren't careful, "Circe" might not take. If one went, they all might, here in the House of Cards. She needed to be shown what was right.

I needed the Jacks. *We* needed them. I had to think about Amaranth. About what we'd need if we had to Forage the nearby farms. If we needed to destroy access roads and overpasses. I didn't know how to cook anything, and neither did Levi.

I scooted out of my chair and ducked into my bedroom. Fluff and Edmund were on the bed, staring with big eyes. Watching things in the darkness that we couldn't even see. I had an old cigar box on my desk, filled with vials of essential oils. It was from my time as a shaman. I'd sketched an eagle's head onto the box's surface with a black marker.

I stepped back into the kitchen and slid the box onto the table. "You're going to clean her up."

Levi stared at the box. "Right. The tub—you two and Penelope. Bathe her. Or something."

"A baptism," Mary said.

Four rubbed her head. "We can't let her go, even if she wants to."

"There isn't anywhere *to* go," Levi said. "Amaranth is all Places now."

Mary lifted the lid on the box. "And these?"

I shrugged. "I don't know. Rub her down with them, or something. It'll look like you know what you're doing."

"Maintain the illusion of control."

They looked at me then.

From up on the roof, I could see most things. The Jacks were inside, having something to eat, while Mary and Four and Penelope worked on Circe. There were still a few beers in the fridge, so Levi parceled them out. He got them started sharing toasts and telling stories. About the school, about themselves, while I kept watch with the binocs. They poured some on the floor, a little bit, every time they toasted.

The pitch of the roof was steep, and I didn't trust the masonry on the old fireplace, so I kept myself in place by holding on to the PVC bathroom vent. One of the women, Four maybe, was singing, down there, below, in the waters. Like something from some Old Country. A *rusalka*, maybe. A tune for the divining pond that could get you underground, where all magic occurred.

I was glad the gas line was still working, because otherwise it would have been a damn cold bath without the water heater.

I could see charred rooflines downtown. The courthouse itself looked like it had been firebombed—the dome at its top, at least. If there was still a Group there, they were staying put. I guessed they went underground, into the service tunnels and storm drains. Salvage had maps for those, which were easy to get. Levi and I had even had a look around ourselves. Before. Dozens of taggers had marked those tunnels. Staking claim. Bullshit like that.

In the other direction, over the backyard, across the bambooed Humvee and the tarped trucks—beyond the apartment building on the other side of the sycamore trees at the edge of the property line, behind Mary's building—I could see a few dormer windows in the mansions along Greek Row. Where the frats were. They were idiots for burning lights upstairs like that, but those buildings were almost impenetrable. And they had more Members than we did. There were more of them who needed to find their way through the darkness and all of the smoke. More worming their ways through the holes in the earth, so maybe it made sense. To beckon.

I could see a bit of the Dallas glow. Not the buildings or the fires themselves—the roof wasn't high enough for that. Elsewhere, in Slade, the Salvage Clearing burned. Clusters of houses and strip malls and unfinished developments were going up as planned. Flushing Outsiders from one place to another—eventually, to be shooed out of Slade altogether. The fires made pillars of smoke that I could only see as black-on-black distortion. Darkness inside against darkness out. But the fires, themselves, like glowing flowers in the darkness—things that couldn't die—those came from the underworld. Amaranths, all of them, as they shone behind tree lines.

Levi made his way up to me. Circe was finally crying down the pipe. I assumed. I could hear something electric buzzing.

"What the hell is that noise?" I asked.

"Tattoo gun. Penelope had it—one of those rigs made from ballpoint pens and a tape deck motor. I think it uses a compass for a needle. You know, like, from geometry classes."

"How the hell is she powering it?"

"Car battery."

"Jesus. What are they tattooing?"

He shrugged. "I need to Hear what happened."

Yeah.

A review. Just in case. Party Leadership wasn't a permanent assignment, and it needed to be reviewed, for future consideration.

But I could only footnote it for him, because minute-by-minute, the more I thought about the operation, the more sense it was making, the more *right* it was becoming.

"Two," Section "I," Subsection "c," "Procedure I.," "The First Phase," Paragraph 1, Item iii.

"And at which point did you lose control?" he asked.

"Two," Section "I," Subsection "c," "Procedure I.," "The First Phase," Paragraph 4, Item ii.

"How did the other Jacks take it?"

"Two," Section "I," Subsection "c," "Procedure I.," "The Second Phase," Paragraph 9.

"What about Mary and Four?"

"Two," Section "I," Subsection "c," "Event Exit Strategy," Paragraph 7, Item viii.

He looked at me then, because we were supposed to always look. "And what about you?"

"Well—" *"Two," Section "I," Subsection "c," "Event Exit Strategy," Paragraph 7, Item iii.*

"Good, then," he said.

He watched the flowers with me, for a time, an arm around my shoulder to steady himself.

"I've seen the Jacks' inventory," he said. "The gains outweigh the losses. The operation was a success."

Some blocks away, people were throwing cocktails at one another. It was beautiful. When car tires screeched, at this distance, it sounded like the hoot of the train that moved through town, late at night, just beyond the city limits. It was a sound I liked.

There was still plenty of gunfire coming from campus, but I hadn't seen evidence of any more Guard. I didn't think there were any more left to come.

"Do I need to explain it again?" he asked.

"No." It hadn't been necessary when I told him I was going west. It hadn't been necessary when we ceased to be a family. It hadn't been necessary when I told my mom and sisters what to do, when this happened, because I wouldn't be coming for them.

I was going to start over.

He gave me a cigarette. We heard something down the pipe.

"To be a fly on the wall in that bathroom right now," he said, staring away.

I laughed. I wondered which of them I would look at most. Which I wanted to look at most.

"At least we found some women," I said. "It was going to be a hell of a sausage fest. Before."

"Well"—he turned and batted his eyes at me—"I guess we would have gone sailor. Taking turns wearing the dress and all that."

I could hear the Jacks, barely, laughing around the table. I guessed they found more beer. Which was all right. We weren't leaving tonight.

We were quiet, while we smoked. It tasted terrible, and it made my head swim.

"Do you remember Charice?" he asked.

"Who?"

"That girl from my biology lab. Went bowling with her."

"Right. What about her?"

"Nothing," he said. "Just asking."

When they brought her out, Circe smelled like sandalwood and amber. She was wearing a white sundress, and they had shorn her hair. I wondered, then, if we should change her name. Bathsheba, perhaps. After all, that name would be in the eye of the beholder— she couldn't take it for herself. Someone had to see her, to lust after her, before she could *become* such. Someone like Luke had done, who could help her bear great children. She had already proven her affinity for explosives. Maybe she had a Solomon in the works, only instead of designing great temples it would blow them apart.

We were looking at her. I even called Matthew and Mark from their post on the porch, keeping watch. Four had come and told me they were bringing her out. It was most important that Matthew and Mark see her. That they saw what Luke no longer could. It had cleared things up for King David, after all—seeing Bathsheba. Mary was holding her hand, standing behind her.

I stood up. "Your sacrifice is ours, Circe."

She looked at me, and smiled. "We will remember him with our first Monument," she said.

I embraced her. Stepped aside so everyone else could. They each laid a hand on her, in turn.

Which *him* did she mean?

And then she lifted her dress and showed us the tattoo—slick with oil, to keep it from scabbing, its india-ink ridges puckered and red over that womb-space between her navel and the low waistband of her underwear. There, the tattoo would expand, become something more, if she ever became pregnant.

. . . *should carry some mark* . . .

The Jacks stared. She stood there, the hem of her dress in one fist, Mary's hand in the other. She stared back.

I looked at the tattoo, at the wildstyle A, with one down-pointed chevron beneath it. Now, when she made grenades, when one of these other boys brought half of the necessary genes and gave her something to carry, she would birth them for us. For Amaranth.

"Hiram," Mark said.

I didn't look away from Circe because, really, I didn't want to.

"We have something for you to read."

I looked then. "What is it?"

He handed me a sheet of paper. "This has to come next. There has to be more."

It was more about the Last Man. They'd written it, I guessed, when I was on the roof with Levi.

Circe lowered her dress.

"We think this is a good time," Mark said. "With Circe's bath and all."

Wearing his goggles, Last discovered fire. He decided to call fire "Prometheus," and he gave it to everyone else.

Prometheus lit the way underground, where Last spent three days measuring the dead. When he returned, with salt and ether, he used glass-water and blood to grow the first woman. We shall name her Last.

Last used ink to spell her name. Everyone else read the letters in the sand.

"Is it good?"

"It's good."

"Can we tag the street with it? For everyone else?"

Merlin had a bottle of vodka among his cook's gear. With permission, he went and got it. Mary took them all, especially Circe, into the living room. Circe followed Mary's examples, mannerisms. She touched the Jacks lightly. She knew what Amaranth could cost, and they needed to know what that felt like, especially at the fingertips of someone beautiful.

Penelope retrieved her tattoo gun, her battery, and the ink . . . *They should carry some mark. . . .*, and she would give it to them. She would write their names in the sand.

I wasn't going to be on watch rotation, so I went to my room. To sleep. Four came with me. She was exhausted, and she didn't have a post in the rotation tonight, either.

We lay in the darkness, listening to the occasional sound of a sentry's footsteps crunching on the gravel drive, outside my window. The cats organized themselves between us.

"How is Circe?" I asked.

"She's fine. For now. She'll be fucked up when she has the chance to. After."

She laughed. "Mary *really* enjoyed bathing her."

I hadn't thought about that.

"Circe's got this . . . thing," Four said. "I don't know. Those boyfriends of hers, they're . . . symptomatic."

I realized, now, that Four had reserved some of the oils for herself. I could smell cedar and vanilla. And body odor. From both of us.

"It's the attention," she said.

I was sure that made some kind of sense.

"By the way, she doesn't want to wear red paint anymore. Is that allowed?"

We didn't actually have rules about paint. About creating oneself in one's own image, with the right color scheme. "Yeah, I guess. What does she want to wear instead?"

"White."

"I see. What about you?"

"I still like black."

I thought for a moment.

Me, too.

"Where did she get that dress?" I asked.

There was a pause. "Christ, Hiram. Don't you think we might pack something other than commando knives and survival blankets? What the hell is the point, otherwise?"

I turned on my side, upsetting Edmund, and offered her a dark smile.

"Did you? Pack something?"

I wondered. Four wore dark shirts, and heavy eyeliner, and jeans with holes and safety pins in them. What would she pack?

What would I?

She wasn't going to answer. I didn't realize until later, trying to fall asleep, how much better than an answer it was. How much better than hearing she had a thong bunched up in her duffel. Or a soft blouse, or dress that would admit sunlight at just the right angle.

"Are you—"

She interrupted me. "What were you going to do before?"

"What?"

"Before. Like, what's your major?"

I thought that it should have been a funny question, but I wasn't laughing. "Interdisciplinary studies."

"Levi, too?"

"Yeah, both of us."

"So what were you going to do?"

"You mean for a job?"

"Or whatever."

I stared at her arm, with its serpents coiling, where I could see her bra strap slipping, in the wan light from the window.

"I didn't have a plan. I didn't know."

"I was going to own my own studio," she said.

"There are acetylene torches and tanks and stuff at Amaranth."

"Where'd you get them?"

"They're just . . . there."

She was quiet for a while, content to smell like vanilla and cedar.

"Can I ask you about your name?"

"Maybe."

"Why 'Hiram'?"

Sitting atop Four's abdomen, Fluff purred. I reached out and stroked her head.

"He was a Phoenician king."

"And that's why?"

"No."

"Then . . . ?"

"When I was a kid, my dad and I built a remote-control robot. It was the first time I'd ever soldered metal before. The first time I'd followed blueprints. I loved it."

Four watched me.

"We named it 'Hiram' because I'd just learned about the king, in Sunday school.

"My dad called me 'Hiram' sometimes—because I spent every waking minute with that thing."

Four smiled. "Do you still have it?"

"No."

THE BOOK:

"THREE"

SEC. "I," SUBSEC. "B" ("MONUMENT")

[1] (i) You should raise your first Monument on "Arrival Day"—under the circumstances, this work does not violate the terms of rest, and you may requisition Members with necessary skills to this end. (ii) Your Monument may take any of a number of forms: an edifice of new beginning, a cenotaph, an expression of the Place itself, etc. (iii) Avoid the use of religious Monuments, for later Additions may not share this faith, which can create division, unrest, and Failure. Religion should, under all circumstances, be a personal event, as should be the maintenance of its paraphernalia. (iv) Do not attach the Place itself to a religion. Doing so invites later fanaticism, which is almost certain to Fail your Place. (v) Do not enforce specific codes of morality. (vi) Do not practice racism, sexism, or other forms of prejudice. Doing so limits the development of prosperity and opportunity without question. (vii) Do not tolerate intolerance.

[2] (i) Your Monument is your Place. It is a version of yourself that resists age and recidivism, insofar as you maintain it. (ii) You must *be* and *think* your Place, and your Place must think *you*. (iii) Your first Monument is your existential compass, and your first Day, in projection, is your last.

"FOUR"

"ADMINISTRATION SCHEMATIC"

[1] (i) With your resource-security apparatus in place, your temporary housing secure, the status of surrounding Groups

and Places mapped, your first Day established, and your first
Monument erected, you must enact your Administration
Schematic. This Schematic must consist of four critical
elements: a civilian militia Leader, a popularly elected
Administrative Senate, term limitation for elected
Administrators, and mandatory militia training for all
Members.

I.A.

"CIVILIAN MILITIA LEADERSHIP"

[1] (i) If you allow your militia Leader to govern his or her
combatants with full autonomy, he or she will eventually
establish a military dictatorship. (ii) To avoid this, make
your militia Leaders accountable to your elected
Administrative Senate. (iii) Militia men and women must swear
loyalty and obedience to the civilian Leadership and to the
Group that sustains them. (iv) In the event that your militia
Leader attempts a coup, he or she must be removed from power
and either banished or executed, as determined by popular
vote. (v) The militia Leader's life is, at all times, in the
Group's hands.

CHAPTER FOURTEEN

"**h**iram," she said gently into the dawn, "wake up."

I was on my side, my ass toward Four. The air in the room was cold—our old heater had been electric, not gas. Beneath the blankets, things were heavy and warm and dark. Four's fingers on my shoulder, where she had planted them to lean into my ear, were heavy and warm. For a time, this place was all places.

"What?"

"Wake up."

"Yeah."

She leaned away and kicked off the blankets. My door was closed—she walked over to it, in her black baby tee and faded-pink underwear. Some of the snakes' eyes, on the back of her arm, were blue. I could see that now. One, though—its eyes were pink, so I stared at her underwear.

"Thanks," she said to the closed door. "We'll be right out."

I heard footsteps leaving.

"Who was that?" I asked, sitting up. I'd slept in my jeans.

"Voice, I think."

I didn't hear him?

"What's up?"

She pulled her jeans over her stubbled legs.

"We have a prisoner."

I watched her dress. It couldn't have been real. This couldn't have been real.

I was seeing what I wanted to.

Matthew and Mark had Zero at gunpoint, on the front porch. They'd bound his hands with the rope that had hanged the cat. They'd beaten the shit out of him.

I thought I'd gotten rid of that rope.

They had him duct-taped to one of the posts supporting the porch. Everyone was assembled.

"We found God," Matthew said, smirking.

Mary and Circe and Penelope were clustered before the door to the 1890s half. Levi leaned against the giant sycamore in the front yard, just below the porch rails. Voice was out in the driveway with Silo, on duty.

I couldn't see where anyone's new tattoos were.

"We caught him trying to leave, last night," Mark said.

Beyond them, in the road, was the new story about the Last Man. They'd tagged it with my wildstyle A. Smoke was climbing slowly, everywhere, like great, gray trees across town. It was very quiet. There were a few people, dead or sleeping, along the sidewalk across Broadway.

"Mary, get the paints, the masks."

"Four, bring me my sword."

. . .

"Look—I just—I'm done."

"You're not done."

"Yes, I am. I won't—I won't—tell anyone. Anything."

"No, you won't."

"I don't want to go west. I'm done."

"You're done."

"Please."

Four looked like she was dressed for a show, wearing her black paint and her black mask.

There was a club in Dallas, a dance club that on Thursdays and Sundays was a retro-goth outfit. I had gone a few times, with Her, after we came back from the west. Before we were done.

I had seen girls there who looked like this. And by that point, I had looked at them, not at Her.

Zero was doughy-faced and freckled. I knew what was coming, so I needed something for him. A history. I imagined that he knew a lot about Ayn Rand, about Objectivism. That he played chess and said almost everything sarcastically. His favorite kind of pornography might have involved women wearing only their shoes.

It was the best I could do.

"You can't *leave*," they said.

They said, "That's, like, spitting on Luke's grave."

"He doesn't have a fucking *grave,* you assholes!" Zero shouted. He was crying. "That's the point! Don't you get it?"

After last night, after the toasts, after Circe and the ink and the names in the sand, Matthew and Mark were taking things seriously. They were the ones who caught Zero trying to leave.

They didn't have many options here. The alternative was not good, and with Circe still around, they had a choice: resent her, or resent something else.

Would Four also take a tattoo? Another one? Would I?

Would she let me see it?

"I just want to go home."

"You know where Amaranth is," I said. "You know we took the Humvee, that we didn't use it to help. On campus."

"You *helped* take the Humvee," Levi said.

"Please."

They needed a sacrifice.

"Where would you go, anyway?"

"Home."

If she were a lesbian, how come Jo had never told stories about her? On the porch, when we smoked out and ate that terrible pasta and talked about "enforcing a sexual politic" and "heteronormativity"?

She told stories about her other lesbian friends, after all.

"Don't you guys want to go back to your parents?"

"Don't ask about our parents."

"To see if they're okay? They *need* us."

"My parents are dead, asshole."

"I hate my father. And my uncle."

"They don't need us."

"Whatever!" Zero said. "What about me? Mine are five fucking miles across town!"

He was spitting as he spoke. Maybe he was good at video games. Had a crush on a girl named Amanda, or Tiffany, or Trish.

Somebody had to pay for Luke's death, and we weren't going to waste the ammunition. The sword *meant* something. You always equipped every first-level fighter, in every campaign, with a longsword. You bought them at Ren Faires, and ordered them from catalogs, because you knew all of their names and measurements, and you thought about those days when men carried swords. When you could still live by your wits, and make communities your own way, with your own rules, because there wasn't a system to keep you down.

"We're going to take a vote, which is the voice of the Group. And then one of you will speak for us. Will give the order one way or the other."

"And the sword?" Matthew asked.

"The sword is mine."

"Eliminate him," Four said.

I hadn't realized, originally, that she was beautiful.

· · ·

"Now cut it down," I said.

Mark spat onto the porch. "Why?"

I looked at him. "Cut. Him. Down."

They obeyed.

"We're going to keep that rope."

Within an hour, we left Slade.

THE BOOK:

"FOUR"

SEC. "I," SUBSEC. "A"
("CIVILIAN MILITIA LEADERSHIP")

(cont'd)

[2] (i) A militia Leader must be permitted to perform his or her job however he or she can. (ii) Militia Leaders must offer full operation transparency to the Administrative Senate (even if a Final Leader serves over them). These reports need not be disclosed to the Group at large. (iii) Your militia Leaders will necessarily order acts of violence, sabotage, and Old Trade inhumanity in the pursuit of Group prosperity.

[3] (i) Though militia service creates a fellowship among its men and women, it is wise to assign certain trustworthy and discreet militia men and women the task of Secret Service. (ii) The Secret Service reports directly to the Administrative Senate.

[4] (i) Your militia must be civilian-led, for military objectives are a means to an end, and never an end themselves.

I.B.

"ADMINISTRATIVE SENATE"

[1] (i) Your Administrative Senate should represent the varied concerns of your Group. (ii) Allow your Members to elect their Senators directly. The use of intermediary voting schematics will generate distrust, which will eventually lead to unrest and Failure.

[2] (i) Make all Senate decisions by majority rule. (ii) If you choose

to elect a Final Leader, the Senate must have the power to overturn his or her decisions with a sufficient majority.

[3] (i) The use of Final Leaders is attractive, and your Group will likely call for one. (ii) Final Leaders are characters of Place, and as such, increase morale.

[4] (i) Any Member should be eligible for election as either Senator or Final Leader. (ii) Do not impose registration fees, taxes, or rites. (iii) Despite your best efforts, any Administration will lead to intermittent frustration and disappointment among your Membership. This is the nature of compromise, and it should be celebrated. (iv) Prosperity arrives piecemeal. Content the frustrated with that. Content yourself with that.

CHAPTER FIFTEEN

In Drop Bay, on Highway 380 (which was a risk we had to take for a while), they had hanged people from trees. My ears were still ringing from the sound of the Humvee's massive tires buzzing across the grooved concrete on the bridge across Lake Bridgeport, on the way into the town. I had burns on my knuckles. We'd broken a roadblock on Highway 209 with the RPG and the .50-caliber. I had to get out of the Humvee to help clear the barricades, after we'd neutralized Them. After we had left them burning.

Mary was riding shotgun with me.

"What's it like?" she asked. "At Amaranth?"

Circe and Silo leaned forward, behind her. They were tasked to the .50-cal, but they wanted to hear, too.

"It has everything we need."

We could see a posse. Between the few main-street buildings in Drop Bay. It moved like a shambling horde.

"We'll do things our way there."

Really, though, it was a mob. Something brainless, that had eaten some of its own extremities to feed the spinal nerve that generated the twitches and shakes that enabled it to *go somewhere*. To do anything at all without a proper brain.

"We'll be safe."

When the woman ran into the street, arms up and screaming, I didn't have any choice. There was a tow truck parked askew on the right side of the two-lane street. I could only go through the left lane, which is where she ran. I would not stop the caravan. I did . . . *not hesitate to use my vehicle as a weapon.* . . .

"Are there trees?"

"Yes, there's an orchard," I said into the walkie-talkie. The other unit was in what had been Penelope's truck, with Four and Penelope and Voice. Voice was driving because Penelope didn't want to, and Four wasn't primary, so we couldn't give her a truck. Voice was bringing up the rear because, save for the Humvee, that truck was the most powerful.

We got intel, over the walkie-talkies, on Channel 19, about an ambush along Highway 83 in Meermont. Where the highway ran through town, they called it "Broadway." We knew there was one on 6, too, back the other way, up and around, because some 'caster had left a small rig with a generator on the roof of a rest stop. It repeated the news, over and over.

Before then, it had been quiet, on all channels. I think that was what interested Truck 12 in talking. In also asking about the trees. In hearing someone other than themselves as we drove toward the towering clouds. West, west.

We wanted it to sound like we had more than four trucks, in case anyone was listening, so we called that one "12."

"Where will we all stay?" Four asked. She was copiloting. Penelope hadn't wanted much to do with her truck since she'd surrendered it to the Group.

"We'll have rooms," I said. "There're rooms."

The ambushes were not Salvage. They were not Party. They were mob, which is why Salvage would tell itself about them. This was not Salvage country, it was just something in the way, a wandering consideration as Places did their thinking, sounding distances to their Members across the collective unconscious of the Salvage hive-mind. It was a dark spot in the synaptic ribbon.

There was silence for a time. Then Four asked, "Who will assign the quarters?"

I smiled.

We stopped in Reign and bivouacked along the loading bays of the municipal post office. We had hoped to get as far as Snyder before stopping, but the Humvee burned fuel faster than I expected. We picked Snyder because we weren't taking a direct route. Too much time on the same highway could lower our guard, we knew.

We were still about two hours from our second-place: a lay-in, in case we needed it. An old Project Nike facility. We had plenty of intel on it. It had Outsiders, already, as best we could tell, but it was worth the risk. That facility could weather anything we might need it to. The clouds were becoming more fierce, out west, and their green underbellies meant they were carrying hail. When I'd been out here, when I'd followed Her and learned about Amaranth without realizing it, I came to know dust storms. If there was one, it would be behind the storm clouds, chasing. Being dragged.

We didn't see many people in town as we drove through, but I wasn't taking any chances. I let Circe and Silo expend a few rounds tearing apart the chain-link fence that secured the post office's motor yard. It was unnecessary, but the sound might keep people away.

• • •

Even in North Texas, which is its own kind of Texas—just like South and East and West, or the Hill Country, or the Panhandle— even there, we got the storms. I would stand with my dad on our porch, listening to the civil alert sirens and watching the rain blow sideways. It didn't matter if a tornado tried to suck us up, to draw us in. Because it couldn't. My father wouldn't let it. So I watched the green clouds spin while he smoked his pipe.

The motor yard's fuel pump had plenty to offer. If there'd been any hoarding, or any runs out here, I'm sure the people went straight to their few gas stations. Or, more likely, all these farm- ers had their own drums full of stabilized diesel and gasoline. They were usually as prepared as Salvage. For anything.

Only Four and Penelope and I were not on watch. Levi had one squad, and Mary had the other, patrolling the premises as we refueled the convoy.

The back doors of some of the postal Jeeps weren't locked. Four opened a mailbag.

Mostly, all she found were bills, but while I watched, she pulled something strange out of the sack. It was some kind of religious scam. There was a foldout paper "prayer mat." You were supposed to kneel on it and pray for fortune. And if you were chair-bound, or couldn't kneel, draping it over your knees would work "just as well."

There was a large picture of a Caucasian Jesus, in some baroque printed frame. You could see the dots of color that whatever bull- shit cheap printer had used to form the image. It was like looking at an old comic book.

We laughed at it. I wondered if the operation mailing these

things out was like Fat Chance. If the ten-dollar "Love Offering" you were supposed to mail in (to cover print costs for the mats, as well as postage for further outreach) had funded some Group's palisade. Some diesel-powered work lights. A few carbines, or rain barrels, or bottles of whiskey.

Levi's party shot at something, but I could hear their laughter. Everything was fine.

"We know so little about them," Four said, folding up the mat and cramming it into my pocket.

"Who?"

"The Jacks."

"We'll know them soon enough," I said.

The pumping diesel fumed between us.

"More importantly"—*and much worse*—"I know so little about you," I said.

"But you know Mary," she said.

I looked over my shoulder and snorted. The Jacks in Mary's squad still remembered that dark office in the bookstore along Meyer Street. They remembered White Mary in the darkness, making everything all right, when the first of them had killed for her. She was Mary, all right. They followed her like dogs, and she touched their faces and told them that what they were doing was right.

But she owed us everything. And she knew it.

What I knew about her, Before, didn't matter of course. It would be better if I didn't know anything about anyone.

"I know enough."

Four walked far enough away to light a cigarette without blowing us up.

"Me, too."

• • •

I was about to call them back anyway, when Matthew and Mark lifted one of the loading bay doors. They had a woman between them. Circe followed behind, the muzzle of one of her pistols jammed between the woman's shoulder blades. Mary followed last, her eyes on everything around her squad.

"What's this?" Four asked. She ground her cigarette underfoot and came to stand beside me.

"Penelope, get that launcher armed," I said.

"Yes, sir."

"Take up a position between Trucks Eight and Twelve, in case we need a diversion."

Matthew and Mark came to a halt about six feet away. They looked proud, but they were looking at Mary. Waiting for some cue.

Mary trailed a finger over the woman's head as she walked past and took up position on my other side.

"She's petitioning for Addition."

"Let her go," I told the Jacks. "Go bring Levi up to speed. Order him back."

They looked at Mary.

"Do it now," I said. "Or I'll let her go for you."

They went. I glanced over at Penelope. She was set up. I smiled when I saw Edmund stand up on his back legs, safe beneath the shell on Truck 12, and peer out the window. I saw him meow silently.

"Did you find out?" I asked Mary.

"Yes," she said. "No dietary, no medical, but she has a son, a twelve-year-old, who is allergic to peanuts."

The woman was dirty. Her clothes were torn. She had dirt in the folds in her skin, which is the opposite of what happened when you wore paint: The folds always ended up clean, unpainted. I couldn't tell if there were highlights in her hair, or if it was streaked with gray.

She wore a tiny golden crucifix on a delicate chain.

I gestured at Mary. She took up position behind the woman. Weapon raised.

"How did you find us?" I asked.

"Please—" she said.

Mary chambered a round in her pistol.

"Answer the questions."

"I just . . . followed you, off the highway."

"You have a son."

"Yes. We've been running."

"Where is he?"

"Hiding."

I looked at the now open loading bay door. At the line of mimosa trees along the southern fence. At the postal Jeeps in neat rows between us and the trees.

"Tell him it's okay. Tell him to come out."

She looked at me for a minute. I knew what she was seeing—young people, probably scared. She wouldn't have approached until she got a look at Mary, watching the perimeter.

She called to him, and he came. Cargo pants, flat-top haircut. He had lacerations on his face, probably from running through greenbrier or something. He stood next to his mother.

I nodded at Mary. She adjusted her aim. Pointed her gun at the boy.

"Please," the woman said.

"It's a precaution," I allowed Mary to say. "In case this is a trap. Is your son a price worth paying? For an ambush?"

Bloody Mary. After so much time sounding distance in the dark before mirrors I couldn't see.

Just in time.

The woman cried, holding her son's hand. He just stared at me.

"Who are you running from?"

"I—I don't know. There are a lot of them. Men. They have a place somewhere . . . around. They have my sister, our car. My husband."

I wasn't worried about Levi. If there was a gang, Levi had the gear to make them burn.

I looked at her son. He wasn't big. He was shaped like I had been at that age—tall, skinny. Sharp elbows and temples and fingerbones. He could be trained. He had probably been in the seventh grade. Before.

"What can you do?" I asked her.

She tucked her hair behind her ears. Cried a little less.

"I can cook. I know first aid. I know a lot about herbs."

"What can you do with these herbs?"

"Lots of things." She looked hopeful now.

Had she also ground strange things in ceramic bowls? Here in the Bible Belt? Had she wondered *What the fuck is going on?* Wondered why copal resin had more *soul* than frankincense? Wondered what to do with asafetida? With Dragon's Blood oil? How to be a shaman, or what was so cool about pagans?

I looked at her crucifix. There'd been a time when I wore one, too—only, mine was just a cross. There'd been no little body of Jesus upon it. We were Baptists, after all. The cross was more important than the Christ.

"Things you wouldn't expect," she said. "That you wouldn't know."

What were you supposed to do with so much witch hazel?

I pulled the Jesus-paper out of my pocket and handed it to her. It was something, at least.

"Try me," I said.

THE BOOK:

"FOUR"

SEC. "I," SUBSEC. "C" ("TERM LIMITATION")

[1] (i) Limit the length of the terms of your Senators and Final
Leader. (ii) Punish those who do not relinquish their terms
when they expire.

[2] (i) Militia Leaders are appointed by the Administration. As
such, they are not elected and are not subject to term
limitation.

I.D.

"MANDATORY MILITIA TRAINING"

[1] (i) All physically and mentally capable Members must undergo
mandatory militia training. (ii) Further, all Members must
provide themselves (or be provided) with arms. (iii) The
reasoning behind this is twofold:

    (a) Should the Place come under attack, your militia may
not be sufficient in and of itself.

    (b) It will likely become necessary at some point for
your civilian Membership to forcibly remove its
Administrators, Administrations, or militia
Leaders.

  (iv) Forbid the use of arms in the settling of differences
between Members, militia men and women, or between the
militia and the civilian Membership. Punish such crimes
severely. Assault upon another Member is a banishment-
inducing offense.

[2](i) Forbid the organization and congregation of paramilitia
groups. (ii) Allow and encourage nonviolent demonstration.

(iii) Allow and encourage public debates, meetings, and reports.

"FIVE"

"ADDITIONS AND RECRUITMENT"

[1] (i) In the early period after your Arrival, you will have to rely on recruiters to secure worthwhile Additions to your Group. (ii) In time, as your Narrative expands into surrounding territories, Addition-seekers will, instead, come to you. Under these circumstances, you can reassign your recruiters to general intelligence gathering.

[2] (i) Recruitment and Addition will become vital to your prosperity for several reasons:

    (a) The larger your Group, the larger, faster, and more effective your resource-security, engineering, and defense programs.

    (b) The sooner these programs become self-sufficient, the sooner you can relegate Members with other beneficial skill sets to other, full-time tasks.

    (c) The sooner you can expand these full-time nonrotating assignments, the sooner your Place will develop professionals, which will add to the prosperity of your Place.

CHAPTER SIXTEEN

In the desert, you think about water. About the fields of dew-traps these Outsiders, these "moles," had dug, to harvest moisture from the air. Alongside the farming plots they'd tilled. The moles whose Place this had been. Now the traps were just funnels of dust in the earth, the collectors under the obscured tarps like so many ant-lions, waiting. The soil rigs in the plots were being re-duned in different directions that better suited the wind, caused by the storm we had finally caught, driving west. The rain had been slight—the clouds weren't ready—but it had been dragging a dust storm.

They were idiots. This shouldn't have been their Place. The storms were no good. It should only have been a stop on the way.

We knew all about this Nike site—about all three parts of it. It was a derelict leftover from Project Nike—a missile defense program from 1950, when we worried about bombers at sixty thousand feet that would bring down the sky. The facilities themselves were much smaller than the larger parts.

Adam and I had traded two fifty-pound bags of flour and a twenty-five-pound bag of salt, which we took from L. D. Pizza, for a manifest of decommissioned facilities like this. It listed coordinates, conditions, current occupants. It used words like *kennel* and *hutch*, and came with a crib sheet for decoding all the terms.

You think about finding water, about keeping it. Creating a society around the maintenance of water. The philosophies and cultures it requires. It is its own way to the underworld, another door to a different immortality—faerie, perhaps. From the Germanic Old Country, the reflecting pools and grottoes and undersea realms. And of course, from Greece. The naiads and the nymphs. Water was a diviner's lens in a bowl with essential oils. Another way to find the animal that is a better you than you.

Water is the collector, the dew-trap at the bottom of the tarp funnel—function as form, the Charybdis waiting. So many ways out. The darkness, the smoke, the holes in the earth. The mirrors and the water. The bullet from the gun in the hands of the mole who'd been ready, down here in the bunker. This was not an underworld because there were no flowers.

This site wasn't far from Amaranth, relatively speaking. It was one of our options, a second-place on our way out. In case we needed one. We knew it would be occupied, like the others, which meant that, if we needed to go there, taking it would be primarily an exercise in vigilance. We hadn't counted on the firepower we had now. We hadn't counted on the Jacks and what they had cooked.

• • •

You think about lakes and reservoirs. About fly-fishing, which is hard. It's an enterprise in the water, a father's rite that sons had to learn. Over our five-day vacation, I caught one rainbow trout, which should have gotten away. In the water, the rubber waders sucked to your legs. A tight fit, a way to be in the water without it knowing, so you could take its fish.

Until, later in the summer, at the same campground, a fifteen-year-old son let the water in by accident, dipping his chest too low to the popping river, to swipe the net at the fish, and the waders became the naiad's kiss, slipping down his chest, dragging him down, down to live dead forever in places with perfect flowers.

Sometimes, it is the sons, and not the fathers, who die.

The first time I saw a dust storm, I was out west with Her. It came upon the horizon like urban smog, a brown thing displacing the sky, a stain that could not be avoided. The red farmer's earth had developed wings, moving in ways that defied normal motion. It swallowed the entire town, dragging it down. You wedged damp towels into doorjambs and window frames, but still your apartment smelled like dust. It smelled cold.

When it was gone, the dirt was piled in drifts like snow. From white to red. Something bloody on something not. Like Mary. Bloody Mary.

You think about Possum Kingdom Lake. Where my grandfather died before I met him, facedown in the water. Bobbing drunk and unconscious and drowning in the hollowed-out floor of the fishing cabin at the end of the pier, under the gooseneck lamps that sucked up the moths. He had a copy of Aristotle's *Poetics* in his pocket. But it's not that simple. That wasn't a philosophy for keeping water.

When the storm started, Levi managed to orient us, using a map and our GPS reader. By the time we were close to the Project Nike site, the storm was upon us.

My father had grown up in the red earth, out here in oil country. He and his brothers chased dust devils and stole produce and killed time. Which is what you did in farm-and-oil country. My grandfather's truck was as silver as silicon. He was a rig man, a pumpjack man, and his truck is what kept him from the dust and the wind, circled with the other company men's trucks—like wagons—to deflect the eddies in the wind that could turn them over. There was never any paint on the trucks because the sand blasted it off. No rust, no blood. No evidence of oil.

The moles' Place housed a broadcast tower, a big, hulking digital thing—the only use that either the government or the private sector still had for the place. We picked up the 'cast on an FCC radio band, and it said "Stay in your homes. Obey law enforcement instruction" over and over and over, co-opting the Salvage repeat. We followed the tower's blinking, bloody lights straight through the storm.

For Salvage, repetition was meaning. Things had to be 'cast, picked up, re-'cast, looped and digitized and taken apart. They had to be jammed and spliced and rearranged so that the same things reappeared, over and over, in different ways. They had to be written, spray-painted, robbed of vowels, glyphed and tattooed.

They had to be burned out of their buildings, *taken* before they could be *stolen*. They had to be the very shirt off your back, so they could be given away, even if someone else had to *give* it for you. Salvage had to be sure that what it heard, what it said, was right. Hearing something, reading something, touching something again and again—as long as everyone else was getting it, too—made it right. Made it real.

If you only said something once, then you were just talking into the darkness, sounding distance. Making noise. Talking to hear yourself speak, like watching mirrors with the lights off.

The moles had an outpost, a converted entry station, but they weren't ready for the fire we brought. In goggles and a mask, Silo opened them up with the .50-caliber, the dust slipping down his torso like water. It splashed into the Humvee, and we breathed through our shirt-masks. Penelope and Voice could handle the RPG well enough, masked against the storm. Mary gave them fire, with Luke's grenade launcher, and Circe's bombs took things apart.

This was how we made that Wall message real.

Merlin had learned to handle the nerve-agent cannon. Once through the outpost, we circled the caravan around the bunker's bay doors, the massive elevator doors in the earth that took big things down or let missiles go up. We circled the trucks against the wind, like my grandfather had, and when Levi opened the door to the service stairs—for going underground and operating the elevator—Zero filled the Place with clouds of nerve agent.

It couldn't have been real, but I made it so. Because we had fire, because we'd gone after the Humvee, to keep it from being real, we fucked ourselves from the get-go. Fore-damned. Fated.

I ordered the descent, waiting with Mary and Silo and Circe

in the Humvee as Levi took the rest to secure the Place. The vehicles swayed as the wind got under them. We couldn't see the lights on the tower anymore.

Which made it my fault.

They cleared the moles out, with knives and the swords, to save ammunition. They kicked aside broken glass, let it swim on the concrete in the vinegar it had held, the preserved vegetables inside limp and colorless and exposed now. Tiny clouds of pickling spice, spilled from their canisters, climbed toward the gap between the bay doors so far overhead, drawn upward by the sucking winds, defying the rules of normal motion.

They piled the corpsed moles on the elevator, which still worked—a massive thing that we would use to bring down some of the caravan. They gave the moles to the wind, lifting dead things to the sky, in the storm. Like rabbis lifting golems, offering them up to receive the Breath of Life—the dust and the wind that began it all. They offered the moles to the red dirt, which is all *Adam* ever meant in Hebrew anyway. *Red,* from the God-breathed dirt that made him. The First Man in all this, before Mary, before the blood. Before anyone had to be sacrificed.

The truth is, we knew that "darkness was upon the face of the deep." That when we followed people into the darkness—into the dust, the smoke, the holes in the earth—that it was a form of drowning. We knew Charybdis would be dark, down below. That when we thought about drawing things in—into our coffer in the fort; into our wide, blue eyes in that parking lot in Slade; into dew-traps or rain barrels—we wouldn't be able to force them back out. Currents only go one way, just like the Spirit of God, moving upon the face of the waters.

There was never going to be any return trip. I didn't enjoy

that week in the river, fly-fishing. I never knew my grandfather, so I couldn't care that he drowned.

The Jacks lifted all the corpses with the elevator, including the one with the mask who'd run from the outpost when we opened fire. The one who was ready with a mask of his own, who had the bullet in his gun, waiting, waiting for the first one down the stairs.

Levi was the first one down, so he took the mole's bullet through his neck. This was as close as he came to the Promised Land—a view across the River Jordan of those dusty, red Canaanite hills. God had fucked Moses over, too, for hitting that rock instead of talking to it. For its water. The Israelites had never had a philosophy for keeping water—for keeping resources—so they had to draw everything they needed from the sky, from rocks, from the people who already lived in the Promised Land. They had to take everything from somebody else.

Everyone always forgets that God parted the River Jordan, too. But only after the right people had died.

When we weren't transcribing 'casts or updating inventories, or training on wooden dummies, Levi and I had made other Plans. Like sailing.

We wanted to sail, because that's what our Romantic idols and fantasy-book heroes did. He inherited a twelve-foot daysailer in bad repair, which we stored at my mother's house. It was only designed for one person, but we would both fit. That was the Plan. Some summer, we'd repair it. Get it ready. Be nothing but flotsam as the wind moved us in ways that defied normal motion.

• • •

The mole gave Levi a way out—to find amaranths underground—with the bullet in that gun. Ahead of his time, ahead of the classic Greeks whom he could finally talk to. Ahead of their relatives listening to gibberish at Delphi. Listening to repeated things from the future, from seventh graders in classrooms. From the intelligence that lay in wait for them to quit being ancient.

By the time Matthew finally flushed that mole out and cut his throat, Levi was already dead.

Last made bricks to build walls for his dead.

The thing about oracles is that they talk back.

I tried to convince myself once, when I was a teenager, that I felt God. Alone in the sanctuary, accompanying my mom on an evening errand to the church. I stared at the ceiling and drew deep breath as quickly as I could. I told our youth minister in his ball cap that I had felt Him. That I was blessed.

But in the end, it was only the wind and the rain, making noise in the darkness.

THE BOOK:

"FIVE" ("ADDITIONS AND RECRUITMENT")

(cont'd)

[3] (i) While your Group grows, so do others. (ii) One of the primary deterrents to assault or Forage is a sufficiently large Group, accompanied by a sufficiently large defense force. (iii) This competition for resource security among groups creates a perpetual-motion phenomenon as all race in size toward Collapse. (iv) This phenomenon is unavoidable, but with careful attention to distrust and unrest among your Group, you can delay such Failure such that your Group yet exists while others Collapse. (v) As others Collapse, your Group may Forage their lives and resources. (vi) When no significantly sized Group exists within range to oppose yours, Failure recovery will be faster and simpler.

[4] (i) The precise skills and abilities you will seek in your Additions will be situation-specific. Several you should watch for (and can rarely have too many of) include medical personnel, experienced educators, physical laborers, engineers, tailors, and combatants. Of particular value are either doctors or midwives capable of safely managing births, since procreation is unlikely to decrease, even following the Collapse of Old Trade.

[5] (i) The sooner you can recruit, establish, and support a medical community, the sooner you can enhance your Group in the form of temporary visas. (ii) Seekers of particular professional communities, such as those who wish their children safely born, can exchange goods and materials for the services of your specialist communities and a temporary stay in your Place—a visa. (iii) This reduces the immediate need for and

risk of external Foraging. (iv) This capitalizes on the
energy expenditure of others and conserves your own.

[6] (i) Recruiters who range from the Place to seek Additions
should be capable of and willing to commit acts of violence,
as very often their survival will depend upon it. (ii) Outfit
your recruiters with the best your militia has to offer in
arms, equipment, and armor. (iii) Recruiters should be
effective at personal stealth, and they should be able to
withstand torture, should they be captured by opposition
Groups. (iv) It is advised that recruiters be equipped with
poison or some similar device for eliminating themselves,
lest opposition Groups Forage valuable intelligence from
them.

[7] (i) Recruiters should double as spies and saboteurs. (ii) They
should be personable and should appear trustworthy. (iii)
Only Members with unflagging loyalty to the Group (or whose
loyalty can be ensured by the continued presence of
valuables at your Place) are eligible for this service.

CHAPTER SEVENTEEN

We were in the L part of the Nike site, which had housed the missile magazines. One of three parts to a site like this. The whole of the part was about forty acres, which was plenty of room. The storm hadn't abated. I wasn't ready to leave.

The problem with romance is the occlusion. The tunnel vision, drawing your every gaze downstream, into those other eyes, the flotsam of your better self, your clearer self, along for the ride. It doesn't matter what secrets swirl and bob in the waters beneath you, as you float toward that lady at Delphi, who, you imagined, reading *Mythology,* must have been beautiful. It doesn't matter that Charybdis, with no body, with no form, with only a mouth-as-being, couldn't have been evil, because she lacked the brain for it. It doesn't matter that following the logical course of events, the natural course, always disadvantages someone else, because love, after all, is simply a competition for resources, made infinitely complex and unknowable when squared and cubed and raised to every other emotional exponent—and then layered with sex and society and a bad memory for what those resources were in the first place.

It was our turn to rest. Mine and Four's. We were using an inflatable mattress in one of the old control rooms. A small, cement cube. There were scars on the walls where electrical outlets had been, back during the Project—I saw them before we clicked off our light. We had to share the mattress, which was fine. Everyone did, in turns.

"Are you okay?" Four asked.

But the Other—waiting, waiting, for you to be the first one down, into the darkness, with the immortal flowers and everything everyone ever said, ancient or not, listening to the oracle or not, about love—is, of course, yourself. A wave function that measures everything you want about and for yourself, while necessarily being nothing else, otherwise you would already be this other person. Because it's nice not to be alone.

She was on her side, lying on the serpent arm. I could tell because I could feel her breath, which helped me orient in the darkness. I didn't have maps for girls in dark rooms. I wasn't carrying a compass. These walls were feet-thick cement, for protection from the exhaust of the climbing missiles, if the Guard had to launch them.

"It's nice not to be alone," I said.

· · ·

That's the reason. The problem. The point. The reduction of self to absolute zero—nothing but the quiet in the darkness, like Orpheus on his way down, defying the laws of normal motion.

Four moved closer. I could smell us better, when she came close, stinking in the darkness. Smelling like death and fire and sweat. All the things from the underworld, where you spoke into the darkness, sounding distance the way bats do, trying not to *look back, or you'll lose her.*

"But are you okay?" she asked.

"I saw this coming."

"What?"

"In Slade, on the Wailing Wall."

She touched my face. "Wait, what? You saw, like, a picture?"

"I saw this."

"What is *this*, Hiram?"

"The darkness," I said. "The solitude. Everything."

After we formed our first secret society. After we taught ourselves, adolescents in the woods, to smoke and to write poetry and to be unafraid. After we taught ourselves to revere, above all things, Love, so we could reduce ourselves to absolute zero and no longer feel those every-day adolescent deaths. After we had codified, structured, and mythified our struggle to be Ready for All Things, we learned that our Narrative was a better "we" than "we" were. It was totemic, and we called it a "knighthood."

After these things, everything Collapsed, because the Narrative did not imply a Group—it implied a mob, a collection of individuals, each of us struggling individually not to be alone.

. . .

Four closed the darkness between us. "Tell me what you saw, Hiram."

"How could it have been real?"

"Hiram."

"I saw darkness," I said. "A square, painted black. Nothing. *My* tag was in the corner."

She was quiet for a minute.

"That doesn't mean anything. Your tag was probably a trick of the light."

"There wasn't any light, so I didn't look back because it might have been real. And it was."

"You didn't see anything. You just think you did. You saw what you wanted to see."

"Shut up," I said.

"It doesn't mean anything."

"It meant everything."

Really, we disbanded the knighthood because Jon and I took girlfriends, and for once, when we tried to sound our own distances in the dark, there were people sounding back, and they were girls. Which made it difficult to believe that our knighthood was real.

We didn't have time for rites in the woods, or Friday nights at Adam's, to game until four in the morning. The feeling of someone's flesh other than our own, beneath our fingers—the sensation of small places between lips and eyelids. These were new physics, and they meant everything more than everything else.

It was Collapse, and it was better than everything that came before it. Than everybody. It was the Event.

• • •

"Hush," Four said.

Her lips were chapped where she pressed them against my nose. A kiss so barely happening, it was the only thought in the darkness. She kissed the way moths might, when there isn't a lamp sucking at them, a Charybdis with no teeth. With nothing but heat and light—what would be left when they dropped the bombs and the Nikes weren't fast enough. When the blasted earth developed wings and fluttered toward the fires in ways that defied normal motion. In ways that couldn't be real.

Four's kiss was bomb physics against my nose. It was ground zero in the darkness, and we'd been pushed into the underworld, through the smoke, underwater—before we'd even seen the flash.

Because that's how it would go.

This was not Collapse. This was something else.

I let the kiss think me.

We'd told ourselves how it would go, how things would remain, when our ideas about love were still soft, because we couldn't afford what it would do to us to cross that Rubicon. There was no going back once you set up the hardware and put the final edges on your ideas about love and sharpness. Then, you were ready, terribly.

Adam graduated a year before I did, and he went away, to Slade. To school. The Plan had been that I would come a year later, after Jon and I graduated. Jon wasn't going to school. He had other plans, and he married the girl who bore his son.

• • •

Four was so close, her lips a moth's wing from mine. Her labret the only thing between us. This was something else, at least.

I spoke into her mouth: "I thought you . . . liked girls."

"I do."

"But—"

She spoke quietly. "I like boys, too. Moron."

Oh.

It was nice to not be alone. We had found a way out, Four and I. One of many that included holes in the earth, columns of smoke, underwater fairylands, and whirlpools with teeth. That included the guns and the noose and the roadside bomb in Irby. Which had malfunctioned and blown apart its crew before we were in range.

It included the bullet from the gun in the hands of the mole who'd been ready. Down here, in the bunker. Waiting, waiting for the first down the stairs.

We'd had . . . *a Plan* . . . , and it included . . . *a Place, a Group, and an Event Exit Strategy. . . .* , to get out, to make it to Slade. To keep our adolescent Narratives alive.

But I hadn't followed it. I went west, following Her, and when I finally returned from the desert, another year later, I could see in Adam's eyes what it had meant to him to be Secondary.

THE BOOK:

"SIX" ("POLICING, MILITIA SERVICE, AND THE NECESSARY LIES OF PROSPERITY")

SEC. "I" ("POLICING")

[1] (i) When your Group reaches sufficient size that you need a system of law enforcement, your police force must comprise civilians. (ii) Do not use your militia to police your civilians. (iii) Situate informants within your police force to ensure it does not abuse your civilian Membership. (iv) Disclose all policing activities to your Group. (v) Do not use excessive force.

II.

"MILITIA SERVICE"

[1] (i) Avoid the implementation of a full, professional army for as long as possible. With professional armies come the risk of military coups. Instead, rely upon a civilian militia, and employ an elite, professional officers' corps. (ii) Determine the length of rotational service in your militia by popular vote. (iii) When rotated out of service, militia men and women should immediately assume some other form of contribution. In this fashion, you anchor your potentially internally dangerous militia to the Place and its Members by keeping them Members and not para-Member enforcers. (iv) Rely upon a volunteer militia for as long as you can. (v) When this is no longer sufficient, you must resort to conscription.

III.

"THE NECESSARY LIES OF PROSPERITY"

[1] (i) Ensuring Group and Place prosperity, especially in the presence of nearby opposition groups, necessitates a number of deceptions. (ii) For example, when opposition Groups become intolerably capable of harming your Group, they necessitate elimination and Forage—even when they have yet to commit any offense against your Group. (iii) Your Group is everything. (iv) Your Place is all Places.

[2] (i) Your civilian Membership will, most certainly, oppose preemptive strikes, acts of sabotage, assassinations, and the like. This is a mark of your new civilization. (ii) To avoid confrontations between the Group and its Administration, ensure that you devote appropriate time, energy, and resources to effecting the deceptions, the blame-placement, and the counter-Narratives that will draw the support of the Administrated for the necessary operations of prosperity.

[3] (i) Prosperity requires such deceptions; however, ensure that such operations are always targeted *beyond* your Place and Membership. (ii) Targeting such operation inward leads immediately to Collapse and Failure, for your armed citizenry will remove you. As you would also do. As you *should* also do. As is always done.

[4] (i) Your Place is an edifice of entropy. (ii) All maneuvers and operations lead eventually to Warfare and Failure. This is inevitable. (iii) Struggle not against Failure; struggle instead to facilitate the most rapid Recovery you can.

CHAPTER EIGHTEEN

I halted the caravan on the Farm Market Road. Outside the gates to Amaranth. I let them look. All of them—even our Addition, Mona (who accidentally revealed her old name), and her son, Levi. I hadn't given him the right to choose a name for himself. I hadn't given Mona the right, either. The boy became our first Monument, flat-topped and unafraid, watching as I cleaned my pistol that morning, before we left the second-place. I told him that I would do anything I had to. To keep him and his mother safe. When I asked him if he understood, he said "Yes."

I told her to expect horrible things, as Four painted my face. We were going masked, for the final leg. All of us. I told them it was just a precaution.

I let them look at the tilled fields, at the pair of modular homes, at the modified single-wides just in front of us, alongside the road. I let them look at the greenhouses and the chicken coop and the goat pen. At the garage and the corrugated-tin workshop.

I let them look at the few homes nearby.

I had brought them through the desert. They were excited, chattering across the walkie-talkies while their trucks idled. Out here, it was quiet. There were no burning buildings, no gunfights. No executions, deaths, accidents. There were no dead husbands or mothers, fathers, boyfriends. There were no abandoned sisters, no credit card payments. This was something that hadn't lied to them, that had drawn them in. There would be no going against the current on the formless waters. Here, there were flowers in the underworld, in the darkness. There was no need to look back, because they weren't trying to get anyone out.

"It's perfect," one of them said into a walkie-talkie. I couldn't tell who it was.

Four rested her fingers on my arm as she leaned across me, struggling to See Everything.

"We haven't Arrived," I said.

They watched, waiting on Mary's orders now, as I got out and walked through the gate. I walked along the driveway, and my cousin came out of one of the homes, a shotgun over his shoulder. The rest of his family peered out at us through the blinds on their windows.

I pulled off my mask.

He leaned the gun up against one of the beams supporting his porch, and they watched him meet me in the caliche driveway.

Mary had her orders, knew when to move in. She was waiting. She was answering their questions over the walkie-talkie. She was telling them because they needed to hear. To see the Place thinking. To see where we would erect the Monument, the underworld mile marker, for our dead.

Last made bricks to build walls for his dead.

They saw me make the offer to my cousin. Saw him using my name, only once. Talking into the darkness to hear himself speak. Making noise. They saw him getting angry.

They saw me lift my Beretta.

"What you did was right," she said.

A CONVERSATION WITH THE AUTHOR

MAKING SENSE OF ALL THIS *NOISE*

Spectra: Allow me to introduce Darin Bradley, author of *Noise*. This novel offers many ideas about individuals, society, and collapse, so I'm going to do my best to make him answer a few questions.

I'm going to jump right into it: Do you really see the near future being this bleak, or did you just have a scary idea and decide to roll with it?

Darin Bradley: Well, I am probably one of the least-qualified people to make predictions regarding the socioeconomic future of the United States. Before I drafted *Noise,* I did a fair bit of research, and as I came to each new stage of revision, I updated the data I'd collected, but even so, I know comparatively little about such things. It's certainly possible that we'll see an "Event" in our lifetimes, but it's equally as possible that this is yet another panicked flash-in-the-pan and that a new status quo and new ideas about "stability" will arise. People have been fearing, discussing, and mythologizing the collapse of their civilizations since the beginning, so our current anxieties may simply be the same old act on a new stage. When you gather in groups, personal fears come to both define and be defined by cultural narrative, so fear of death—of the End of All Things—necessarily occupies large portions of our senses of self.

But, I think we can agree that "collapse" or "apocalypse" is definitely in the air. Today, it may be the quickest shorthand for the global zeitgeist.

As for the novel, I'd say it was a coincidence that the story came to mirror, in many ways, what's happening around us "right now" (which is about a year before *Noise* was printed). That's the short answer, but as a participant in *this* cultural narrative, I was almost certainly channeling some of what was going unsaid in the American hive-mind.

The story itself arose from years of thinking about social theory and only came to be because of the situation I found myself in: I had just finished my Ph.D. in English literature and theory, I didn't have a job, and my wife and I had moved from Texas to South Carolina. Suddenly, I didn't have to be in class anymore, I didn't have to write a dissertation, and I didn't have to teach. So I had a head full of cognitive theory and nineteenth-century American utopianism, and I had loads of free time. This was all in the fall of 2007. I decided on the story I wanted to tell, and that led me to the idea of the *Book*. With the plot in mind, I actually wrote the *Book* first—initially, it was much longer than it is now—and when the economy started quaking in the fall of 2008 (a few months after we'd sold the novel), I was as surprised as anyone.

To come back to your question: I suppose I had a scary idea about loss, and social collapse made a perfect vehicle for arriving at the tenor of that metaphor.

S: One of the reasons I enjoy talking to you is because, like many readers, I like to know about the author (I tend to look at the author photo to get an idea of "who is telling me this story"). I think this is because we want to see if any of the characters in the novel are subtly (or not) a shadow of the author. Would you say any of the characters in *Noise* have any connections to your own life (being aware, of course, that admitting to murder here might be a bad thing)?

DB: Of course, all of the characters are connected to me (*are* me), in that they're all ideas of what people could be like filtered through Hiram's perspectives, anxieties, beliefs, etc. But that's a bit of a dodge. Hiram's story is largely *my* story. Now, I won't entirely say which of his experiences and characteristics are direct self-portraits, but, for example, my father is alive and well (unlike Hiram's). However, I did live in that duplex at that age with a roommate like Adam (the duplex's description, location in town, and its personal importance are all, definitely, lifted straight from my past—it's still there, by the way, in roughly the same condition). Certainly, I've never lived through a social collapse, so I haven't done anything that Hiram does in the novel, but a very large portion of his past experiences, personal mythologies, and perspectives might qualify as narrative nonfiction.

Hiram fascinates me because he is, indeed, my shadow, but he's struggling much harder for clarity, for solidity, than I do (or did). His past tells us that he was a "good" kid, but the wholesome things he learned playing T-ball, or in the Boy Scouts, or at church become very confusing and problematic when their contributions to his identity can no longer serve him. When you can no longer count on inhabiting a generally peaceful and cooperative social environment, things like how to hit a ball off the T, or how to be "loyal," very suddenly come to mean something else. When the mind is desperate to keep itself alive, any past experiences are fair game for deconstruction and revision.

As for Slade—I've renamed some streets, moved some buildings around, and taken artistic license with my descriptions, but otherwise, it's very highly based on the town I was living in at Hiram's age: Denton, Texas. Again, I won't say what's "real" and what's not about the town—you'll just have to pop in for a visit and see for yourself.

S: Hear that, Denton Chamber of Commerce—stock up on brochures! Okay—taking a different tack, what would you say if someone described this book as "a dystopian novel"? Do you find that an accurate genre for *Noise*?

DB: I think it's difficult to say, one way or the other, in regards to the "real world" in the novel. However, the meta-society that Hiram and the gang intend to create at Amaranth very well could be dystopian. They envision an almost totalitarian, certainly fascist, regime. So, from the perspective of a real-world, contemporary U.S. reader, we could say that Amaranth is (or would be) dystopian. However, as far as the characters in the novel are concerned, it *isn't* dystopian—it's *utopian*. At Amaranth, they'll be safe, they'll be free from persecution and predation, and they will acquire everything they need to live *their* way. If one looks back at the utopias of, say, Thomas More, Charles Fourier, or Edward Bellamy, one might conclude that realizing utopia is impossible—but only *sort of*. Whoever ends up at the top can certainly achieve utopia, only *personally* instead of *socially*. History largely tells us that utopian communes fail (e.g., La Réunion near what's now Dallas, or Brisbane's and Greeley's Fourier-inspired "phalanxes," or the Ripleys' Brook Farm), but could you make one succeed as a totalitarian compound, à la the medieval city-state, wherein the civic leader(s) lives in luxury? In a personal utopia? I think you could.

Really, though, for the novel as a whole, you'd need several perspectives to draw a conclusion about utopia, dystopia, or anti-utopia. There is the collapsed world, but then there are the worlds that Groups have established (or will establish). CLO.WN, for example, seems to be in hog heaven, so I'm not sure we can call their society anti-utopian (it's not *striving* to be utopian, it already is—to them). Hiram and his allies, however, spend the entire novel not having "Arrived" at their "Place," so they occupy a non-space—meaning, all we can really classify are their worldviews, not any "real" society. Does this make the novel "dystopian," as far as genre is concerned? I can't say, but really, genre labels are less important than the readers' reaction to the story.

S: Still, I think it isn't a stretch to say that *Noise* follows a similar path to those postmodern post–World War II novels about the collapse of society. I'm specifically thinking of not just *Lord of the Flies* and *1984*, but also the works of J. G. Ballard, such as *High Rise*. Since much of this tradition evolved from the growing political and social systems of the post–World War II, post–Cold War mentalities, how do you explain the anarchy of *Noise*? Do you see society already in this state of regress?

DB: Boy, that's a can of worms. In fact, Hiram hints at it when he hears the newscaster refer to Salvagers as "anarchists" (he wants to hit her).

The role of anarchy in Salvage, it seems to me, is philosophical. To them, Ralph Waldo Emerson and Henry David Thoreau were *the* nineteenth-century American anarchists (though I'm sure there are a few Americanists who would take issue with the idea).

Emerson and Thoreau (and other American Transcendentalists) advocated that no one person can hold authority (moral or legal) over another simply because of the accident of birth. For many, "anarchy" connotes violence, arson, theft, abuse, etc., but this should really be referred to as "omniarchy," which isn't the anarchic idea that "no one rules" but rather that "everyone rules"—which is shorthand for do whatever the hell you want to.

For Salvage, anarchy seems to be the motivating philosophy behind their eagerness for the Event. If they no longer have to fear imprisonment (or worse) for ignoring someone else's ideas about "law" or "morality," then they are free to remake society as they please—to correct the wrongs and traumas they've endured in their lives. Ironically, the *Book* tells us that one must control disposition, morality, and behavior to effect a successful New State, which is about as far from anarchy as possible. (I think this dovetails nicely with what I said before about personal utopias.)

To answer your last question: I don't see society in this state of regress, and I'm not one who believes that philosophical anarchy can "work." It's true that society, law, culture, and even religion form a sort of property-insurance gestalt, which takes a bit of the magic out of what it means to "have" a nationality. Most of our laws, and what we believe about them, are designed to prevent us from enjoying freedoms at someone else's expense, but that makes for a boring national identity.

Certainly, there's a thin line, which Salvage watches for eagerly—the line between a pacified, law-abiding nation and a culture-wide realization that their property is no longer insured by the state—including their own lives—but I don't see that line breaking down anytime soon.

S: That's a relief! The *Book* is definitely one of my favorite aspects of, well, the book, especially as much of this advice seems like it's a very sound plan for getting through a Collapse. Can you explain your process (and, perhaps, your inspiration) for what is essentially a guide to escaping a broken society and forming a new one?

DB: Like I mentioned before, the *Book* came first. I had the story in mind, but I needed to establish the specifics of the Salvage philosophy before I could really explore what that philosophy would mean for the people adhering to it.

So, buckle up—this is going to take a minute.

I began by conceptualizing a proto-nation—a simple survival group—and worked my way backward. That is, I tried to consider things like ethnic conflict, transnational trade, territorialism, religion, politics, and so on. I drew the very simple conclusion (and I'm not the first to do so) that resources (specifically, controlling them) determine everything. Once my proto-nation had found a way to feed itself, find water, and avoid dying from exposure (to the elements or to enemies), it could begin to establish its Narrative, which I see as the next essential step to survival. Without an idea who "we" are, it becomes difficult to determine who is allowed to consume our resources. And if there is no "us," we won't even be able to effectively band together to defend the resources we control.

In my model, if you destabilize the things that underpin civility and humanitarianism, then you can't afford to do the "good" thing and share your resources with anyone in need. Certainly, you *could* share, but ultimately, you'd starve. Essentially, I thought about "humanity" as inconstant—that is, while we typically think that we are ourselves (our identities) all the time, I pursued the idea that we aren't. I mean, when I'm staring at the television, mindlessly, I'm not attending to all of my personal philosophies, fears, anxieties, etc. I'm a little less "me." According to the *Book*, the same principle applies when you're starving, worrying about enemies, or simply spending all day cultivating food. You have less time to consider things like personal religion or philosophy—you are a little less "you" than you are right now, calmly reading these pages. I think we often forget that the things we hold so dear (and that we fight so much about)—like who created the universe or who is allowed to get married to whom—are luxuries that evolved with us only as we banded together and gradually created those free-time opportunities to simply attend to the strange images in our heads. At one point in our history, we certainly cared a lot more about killing and eating things than we did about who might be watching us from the clouds.

Still with me?

S: Still with you.

DB: So, this "inconstant self" thinking enabled me to strip away my conceptual reservations about things like killing someone for his or her food, or preemptively attacking a neighboring community simply because you can't take the risk that they might do it to you first. The *Book* then became an involved set of ideas to facilitate a new cultural Narrative—one that helps define "us versus them," that defines how the cultural world works and what citizens have to do to fit in. It became about maximizing the contributions of each citizen for the strength of the whole. It became about preemptively convincing the "Group" that it is always right and that "Outsiders" are always wrong—in fact, they're inhuman. Which, you know, isn't a revolutionary idea; religion and culture have been struggling for millennia to establish the particular "correctness," the better "person-ness," of one group over another.

So, really, the hardest part was creating a realistic perspective on the complete collapse of civility. After that, I decided that my emphasis would be on personal energy, since in this situation, one would have to constantly replenish it with food, water, and rest. Most of us don't worry about this *right now* because we have ready access to all these things (helping someone push a stalled car out of an intersection is a fine thing to do now—you can replace the lost calories later. But if helping this person meant you'd have less energy to protect yourself from a mugging later, because you couldn't replace the calories or safely rest, would you still help? Many of us would, and we would, in turn, be murdered by people who wouldn't, because we would be weaker than they. I tried to take this idea of "conservation" to its most logical extremes, in an urban setting, and what you see in the *Book* is the result.

S: To follow up on something you mentioned earlier: You were talking about the irony of how the *Book*, although a product of Salvage, is actually advocating a philosophy that seems almost wholly different (anarchy versus organization). Can you go into that a little more?

DB: Sure. The Book is decidedly non-anarchic; it advocates organization, distributions of power, and collective opportunism. In a way, it makes sense that this is what Salvage would have generated: After all, they were creating this rebellious social model as a reaction against what they saw as the failing of free-market capitalism (and the social problems it entails). However, a world organized according to the *Book* depends first upon the collapse of the old model (Old Trade), which would result (Salvage believes) in anarchy. Anarchy is a crime under the old model, and Salvage doesn't want its people tied up in jail, killed by riot police, or otherwise out of the picture before the game even gets started—which is why the *Book* is so clear that it's outlining a *reaction* to anarchy, not a plan to cause it. But, of course, once the Salvage hive-mind really gets going, mob mentality takes over and the *Book* gets (in some ways) misused.

S: One of the key issues in the novel is the idea of renaming and masking. One thing I was wondering, though, is eventually— when Amaranth is firmly established—will they ever go back to their old names? Do you think they even could, if they wanted to? Or, as it is a new society, are these new identities permanent?

DB: I think that depends on whether or not (and how) Amaranth succeeds. If everything goes according to plan (which I don't think it would), and they become a strong, self-sufficient city-state, then the Members might certainly have time to be "more" themselves, like I mentioned above. That would mean, for most, attending to the horrible things they've done and the people they left behind. Retaking their given names would essentially mean reassuming their old identities, which are, morally, the guilty parties in this situation. It seems to me that would be pretty traumatic, and it could quickly drag the city-state out of its success—not everyone would want to revisit the past (I don't think Hiram would), so it would likely create friction between the two groups, especially since the accusation on one side is that their entire lives are lies and that they're just playing the biggest game of pretend ever.

But at the same time, if life is difficult, if there isn't time to sit around and think about what you've done, then it would be less likely that Members would even revisit the issue of their old names (the *Book* is quite against it, and it's certainly the closest thing to a new cultural religion that they have). And, you know, the mind is pretty elastic. It's capable of fascinating maneuvers that protect the body-mind from trauma—that keep it functioning in difficult circumstances. Self-doubt wouldn't be good for survival, so I think whoever was first to want to reclaim his or her old name would likely be made an example of . . . before the trend caught on. Their new identities, after all, protect them from their old ones.

S: Interesting—you don't think Amaranth will succeed? Or simply that it won't go according to plan? Are the two things mutually exclusive?

DB: I wish I could say. When I look at what the *Book* has to say and then compare that against how Hiram and the others interpret it, I can't help but see, in places, a disconnect—the misuse I mentioned before. Clearly, Hiram and his allies follow many of the rules *exactly,* but not *all* of them—and it's important to remember that the version of the *Book* that we see is unique to Hiram and Levi. Undoubtedly, they encountered other rules, suggestions, or directives that they simply didn't envision in *their Book.* What might be missing that we simply can't conceptualize? Which threats or realities are they not prepared for? I thought of a few, which I removed from the *Book* on purpose, but I'm not telling . . . I think that if Amaranth is going to succeed, and if Hiram is going to have the first crack at "Final Leader" (it seems to me that he will), then he needs to learn a few vital lessons very quickly, or he'll die (and possibly get everyone else killed, too). At the end of the novel, he's almost there, but not quite, which is how I wanted to leave him. In a very dark way, it's the closest thing to "hope"—to a redemptive ending—that I can tolerate.

S: Even though your characters struggle with it at points, do you think it would be easy to transition to the violence they engage in? Is that why the ceremony of it is so key?

DB: No, I think it would be very difficult for the vast majority of people. In his book *On Killing*, Lt. Col. Dave Grossman cites the ominously titled WWII study "Combat Neuroses: Development of Combat Exhaustion" by R. L. Swank and W. E. Marchand. Grossman parses the study to reveal that only about 2 percent of combat soldiers are predisposed to be "aggressive psychopaths" and hence do not experience the same reservations about killing that the rest of us (and the rest of most soldiers) do. Until the Vietnam War, when the United States began new programs to overcome a soldier's resistance to killing, most soldiers spent most of their time missing the targets they fired at (both intentionally and subconsciously)—Grossman's book offers some fantastic data regarding this.

Generally, we don't like hurting one another, so, for example, picking up a sword and swinging it at a woman's legs, like Hiram does, would be *incredibly* traumatic. In fact, it's not likely (statistically speaking) to happen, despite whatever stories about toughness we may tell ourselves.

Now, I think that as time goes by and these reservations about violence start to fade in the interest of self-defense and survival, things would change. Violence against Outsiders would become easier—being part of an "us" would give people somewhere productive to channel their humanity while simultaneously becoming more and more irrationally angry at "them." But the initial transition would be so incredibly difficult that most of us wouldn't make it.

As you suggest, this is why Salvage is so adamant about masks and names and narratives. If you're going to survive the

Collapse, Salvage believes, you can't be slow to adjust—you have to become comfortable with harming others *now*. By wearing a mask or war paint or a uniform, you get to be somebody else—and that person is responsible for the violence, not you.

And you know, these ideas aren't particular to Salvage—think about the types of people in our societies who sometimes have to kill others, like law enforcement personnel or soldiers. We change the language—they aren't committing "murder," it's just doing what's "right" for the national interest. We give them uniforms (costumes), ranks, sequestered fellowships, ceremonies, parades, and so forth. We call them by their last names, or by their nicknames. We do everything we can to help them overcome the aversion to violence in an organized fashion. And then we assure them that "what you did was right," to assuage guilt in the hope that they'll do it again.

Don't get me wrong: I'm not making a value judgment—in fact, I have great respect for soldiers and policemen, both of which run in my family—but all of these techniques we employ demonstrate, I think, that we don't like bashing one another with two-by-fours or shoving people off of cliffs or shooting at them.

And maybe that, in the end, is what will redeem us.

S: Is that, ultimately then, what you want people to take away from *Noise*?

DB: No. I won't say that *Noise* has no message (that would be naïve), but I wouldn't cite redemption as a contender. I dislike redemption in literature because it's more often a fairy tale than an aspect of meaningful existence. We may often hope for or seek redemption, but I think it's a rare find, and celebrating (or even portraying it) in fiction feels like a scam.

I think the novel has a lot more to say about personal mythology and the mutability of self. We are each of us masterworks of fiction, nuanced by beautiful and terrible experience and powered by ambition. "Good," "evil," "right," and "wrong" are just frame stories, and they're rarely true.

S: Then, I think it's safe to say this: What you did was right.